Praise for *Of Knights and Books and Falling In Love*

Rita A. Rubin's latest *Of Knights and Books and Falling In Love* is a tale of wit and sentiment that rivals all cosy fantasies and is a notable addition to the collection.

Quinton Li, author of *Tell Me How It Ends*.

Of Knights and Books and Falling in Love is a heartfelt delight. Rubin's writing style is perfectly suited for a slice-of-life tale, and these characters will steal your heart. Look no farther for your next cozy romantic fantasy novel: Rubin's got you covered.

Talli L. Morgan, author of *Meliora*.

Sweet, endearing, and wonderfully charming, with characters that don't shy away from their trauma and a romance that feels deeply well-earned. *Of Knights and Books and Falling In Love* is a slow-burn cozy fantasy that will enchant you.

Amanda Ferreira, author of *Entangled with an Elf Prince*.

A beautifully crafted journey of redemption wrapped in a cozy fantasy that will have you smiling and will make your heart soar. Rita A. Rubin shows the healing powers of romantic and platonic love.

Taylor Hubbard, author of *A Corruption of Souls*.

A nightmare turned daydream. Jayce's happily ever after would melt even the most villainous of hearts.

E.M. Harding, author of *Labours of Stone*.

OF

KNIGHTS

AND BOOKS

AND

FALLING

IN LOVE

Rita A. Rubin

Of Knights and Books and Falling In Love.

© Rita A. Rubin 2023.

Cover illustration by Jan Falk.

Typography by Beauregard River.

ISBN: 978-0-6450928-6-8

Chapter
One

When Jayce returned from a recent battle in the north, he found the Dark Citadel in a state of exhilaration. He would have thought it was because the Hero, their greatest adversary, had finally been defeated.

It turned out to be something *almost* as exciting.

They had captured the Hero's lover.

"Go and speak with our new guest," the Dark Lord—Jayce's master—said to him some time later. The two of them were alone in the Dark Lord's quarters, which were lavish and without a hint of colour for the eye to see—the Dark Lord took his title rather seriously.

He sat opposite Jayce, in a high, wing-backed chair, beside one of the towering, arched windows that overlooked the city surrounding the Citadel, sipping red wine from a crystal-cut glass. His pitch-black hair fell in long, glossy curtains around a face so pale it was almost white.

"I assume you don't want me to simply ask him about the weather?" Jayce asked. His own wine glass remained untouched on the low table between them. He had no intention of drinking it unless his master ordered him to do so.

Jayce's remark drew an amused smile from the Dark Lord's lips. "No. I want you to find out if he knows anything . . . interesting, about the Hero and her forces. Anything that we could use to our advantage."

"I thought we already had the advantage by capturing her lover?"

"We must take any advantage we can get. Even if it is as meagre as a crumb of bread," he explained, his voice soft. Always so soft. Somehow, that made him sound even more sinister. "You should understand that, Grey."

Jayce stifled the shiver that always snaked through his body whenever the Dark Lord used the name he had given Jayce years ago. The tone he used when he spoke Jayce's name made him feel as if invisible fingers were trailing slowly down his spine.

"Of course." Jayce stood from his seat. "I'll go see to the prisoner now."

As he made his way across the black marble floor, towards the doors, he heard the Dark Lord say, "Good boy."

Like the rest of the Dark Lord's castle, the dungeons were carved from obsidian stone. But unlike the rest of the castle, the dungeons were dank and windowless, lit only by the orange glow of torchlight, which set off the shine of the damp on the walls.

Jayce had visited these dungeons on numerous occasions over the years and never for anything pleasant. He was almost certain that no cell down here hadn't had its walls spattered with the blood of an enemy of the Dark Lord at least once before.

"Ah, Grey." A hulk of a man stood in the dungeon corridor before Jayce.

Detlas, general of the Dark Lord's army. He had a face like an ox and an even uglier disposition. He was currently dressed in his spiked black armour, which only added to his imposing figure. Jayce knew that the general had been the one to retrieve the Hero's lover.

"I'm to interrogate our newest guest," Jayce said without preamble. "As per the Dark Lord's request."

"Interrogate, eh? Need me to join in?"

Jayce inwardly grimaced at the eager grin on the man's face. Detlas was the kind of man who seemed only to find pleasure in causing others misery. As sadistic and base a man as they came, it was no surprise to find one such as him in the employ of the Dark Lord.

"No need," said Jayce crisply. "I'm perfectly capable of handling one prisoner myself, but I'll be sure to call you in if there's any cleaning up to be done. Now, take me to him."

Detlas led him all the way down to the cell at the end of the long corridor. Through the thick iron bars, Jayce saw a lone figure sitting slumped against the back wall of the cell, his arms suspended above his head by heavy chains. A young man who looked to be not much older than Jayce himself.

Not much was known about the Hero's lover. What little Jayce did know of him was all second-hand information. He was a knight from Étoisaint, a town to Solière's west, and one of the few places the Dark Lord's war had not managed to touch. Jayce also knew that he was something of a hero in his own right, having helped the Hero to win quite a number of key battles over the years.

He had apparently helped the Hero to slay the basilisc when they retrieved the Sorrow Blade—a powerful weapon instilled with arcane magic. One that the Dark Lord had been most aggrieved to lose to the Hero.

Now, he didn't even stir when the torchlight threw their long shadows over him.

"If he's dead, I'll be very cross with you, Detlas."

The larger man snorted. "He ain't dead. Probably still just knocked out cold. He kept putting up a fight, so my men kept clubbing him over the head."

Jayce opened the cell door, and the prisoner still did not so much as twitch.

"Hm, maybe he is dead," Detlas said.

"For your sake, he better not be." Jayce strode into the cell. "Now leave us."

"Aw c'mon. You could at least let me watch."

He shot Detlas a withering look over his shoulder. "Leave. *Now.*"

The door slammed shut in Detlas's face, startling the general into leaping back a step. Grumbling, Detlas left them, but not before Jayce caught some of his less than pleasant words. "Bitch thinks just because he's the master's pet, he can get away with treating everyone else like dog shit."

Jayce didn't trifle himself with Detlas's words. They weren't among the worst things others had said about him, after all. Instead, he focused on the man in front of him.

"You can stop pretending," he said smoothly. "I know you are awake."

The prisoner lifted his head to catch Jayce in his fierce, dark-eyed gaze. He had skin the colour of mahogany and a head of black, disorderly curls. Thanks to the torchlight spilling in from the corridor, Jayce could see the bloodied cut along his lower lip and the swelling of bruises on his face—one beneath his left eye and the other at the corner of his mouth. There were bloodstains on the front of his tattered undershirt.

Jayce plastered an amicable smile across his face. "There he is. A pleasure to meet you, Sir . . .?"

The man only clenched his jaw and turned his head away defiantly.

Jayce sighed. "Don't be difficult. All I'm asking for is your name. You know my name, don't you?"

The tone in the man's voice was pure venom when he replied, "Grey."

No, came a voice unbidden in the back of his head. Jayce ignored it and said, "Now don't you think it's only polite that I know yours?"

The man only continued to glare.

Jayce let out a bereaved sigh. He'd been hoping he wouldn't have to resort to any unsavoury methods of interrogation. Which, admittedly, had been foolish of him.

He extended his left hand, as if he were reaching out to grab something. The prisoner made a choked sound and his body seized.

Straining against his chains, a low, pained moan slipped past his lips.

"Wh-What are you—"

"Tell me your name," Jayce demanded calmly, even as something churned uncomfortably inside of him when the prisoner's legs started jerking, like he was trying to escape the pain that was inside of him.

The prisoner made another sound that reminded him of a wounded animal.

"Tell me your name," he repeated. "Tell me and I'll make it stop."

The prisoner did an admirable job of resisting before he inevitably relented. In that time, Jayce found himself willing the pain to grow stronger while also willing the prisoner to just give in, so Jayce could stop.

"A-All right," the prisoner ground out. "J-just . . . stop. *Please, stop.*"

Jayce lowered his hand, and the prisoner slumped forward; his ragged gasps sounded overly loud in the confines of the cell.

Perhaps it had been unnecessary to torment him like that for refusing to answer with something as unimportant as his name. However, Jayce thought it better to show their prisoner what failing to comply would lead to. Maybe now that he had had a taste of what Jayce could do to him, he would be more forthcoming with the answers Jayce needed.

"Your name, please."

"A-Alexius," said the prisoner between gasping breaths, "de Viccarri."

"Well, then, it's a pleasure to make your acquaintance, Alexius—"

"Your collar."

Jayce's mouth snapped closed, his hand instinctively came up to the jewel-encrusted, silver choker that covered the entirety of his neck. "What?"

"Your collar," Alexius repeated. "I-I know what it is. It—"

"*Shut up,*" Jayce hissed.

But Alexius was either incredibly stubborn, or incredibly foolish— or both, really—because he ignored Jayce's warning and kept speaking. "I've seen one just like it before. I know what they do, they . . ." he frowned. "You're being controlled, aren't you?"

Faster than either of them could blink, Jayce moved forward until he had Alexius by the throat, his grip hard enough that he heard the young man let out a strangled cough. "I said, *shut up*."

The damn fool wouldn't let up, even with Jayce cutting off his airways. "My-My father was a professor. H-He studied these kinds of things . . . I—I could—"

"Gods, do you *want* me to kill you?"

Impossibly, a smug grin curled at the corner of Alexius's lips. "Would you?" he rasped. "If I told you I knew how to remove it?"

Jayce dropped his hand as if burned. He backed away from Alexius as the other man coughed and sputtered. The beat of Jayce's own heart felt too loud to his own ears. He hated the notion that this stranger might know of the collar and what it did to Jayce. Hated that he might just be toying with Jayce by saying he knew how to remove it.

"We're done here," he said, and swept out of the cell before he could allow anymore of his composure to slip away from him.

There were bits and pieces that Jayce still remembered from his life before he came into the service of the Dark Lord. He remembered an apple orchard, running through the sun-dappled paths that snaked between the trees. Picking out the reddest and juiciest apples whenever he wanted, biting into them and savouring the explosion of sweetness on his tongue.

He remembered a small, brown puppy curling up with him by a lit fire. He remembered his mother singing.

And he remembered being in the city of Redvale with one of his mother's workers on the day the Dark Lord's forces took it.

Jayce could still hear the screams. See the chaos and destruction. Still feel the fear that rushed through him at the time. He still remembered with crystal-clear clarity when the man who had told Jayce's mother he would take care of him, was cut down by one of

6

the Dark Lord's soldiers. The horrible sound he made when the sword went through his back and came out of his chest. The terrible expression on his face and the red of his blood.

Jayce had been spared that day only because the Dark Lord himself had taken one look at him—a terrified and snivelling boy—and seen something in him. Something worthy of taking Jayce in and training him over the next five years to become his apprentice. His servant, his successor. His lapdog. To become one of the most fearsome men in all of Solière.

And to ensure this soft-hearted boy, who he had spent so much time trying to mould into his perfect successor, would never rebel against him, the Dark Lord had stuck a collar on him.

The hour was late when Jayce stood in his rooms before a body-length mirror propped up on the wall. He looked at himself reflected in the clear glass. A tall man of twenty-two, slim build hidden beneath swathes of black and silver robes. Pale skinned with long hair that fell past his shoulders in strands of silver. Black markings traced the line of both of his cheekbones.

There were only two points of colour on Jayce's person. His eyes, the colour of aqua gemstones, and the three garnets embedded into the silver collar around his neck. One of which was almost as big as his palm.

He touched the collar, watching his reflection as he brushed his fingers against the stones and ornate metal. One might look at it and think it a beautiful piece of craftsmanship. May see it as nothing less than a stunning piece of jewellery.

To Jayce, however, the sight of it was detestable.

The Dark Lord had put it around his neck when he was only twelve and it had not come off since. Could not come off, as Jayce knew all too well.

While the collar imbued Jayce with some of the Dark Lord's power, it also gave him complete control over Jayce. It ensured that whatever his request, Jayce could never refuse. No matter how cruel or vile, if the Dark Lord wished it, Jayce would see it done.

It was also a symbol of the Dark Lord's ownership over him. A reminder that Jayce was a tool. A *possession*.

He *hated* the fucking thing. How he wished he could wrap his fingers around it and tear the collar off.

"I know how to take it off."

This collar was powerful, arcane magic. Was it true that this Alexius, this man who was supposed to be his enemy, knew the secrets that even Jayce did not?

What if he's simply lying? he asked himself.

And if he isn't? What do you really have to lose here? Other than an opportunity to finally be free of the Dark Lord, should you choose to not heed this man's words?

~

Jayce returned to the dungeons early the next morning. The prisoner—Alexius—was still in chains against the back wall, his head hung low. When Jayce opened the door to his cell, however, he lifted his head immediately, eyeing Jayce with both surprise and wariness.

"Tell me how to get the damn thing off."

Chapter
Two

It was foolish.

It was mad.

Perhaps the most foolish and mad thing he'd ever done.

But if this reckless gambit paid off, it would mean Jayce would finally have his freedom back. It made the thought of potentially being caught and tortured on pain of death, worth it.

Alexius de Viccarri was willing to help Jayce take back his freedom, but he had a few conditions that he wanted met first.

"I can tell you what I know about the collar and how to get it off," he told Jayce. "But I want my freedom back as well."

"You want me to help you escape?" said Jayce.

Alexius nodded.

"Unfortunately, that's going to be quite impossible."

"Why? I know you being here and talking to me about this must be disobeying your master's orders. So what is stopping you from simply throwing me the key and letting me do the rest?"

"Because I've been told to interrogate you and glean any information I can off of you. I can't exactly do that if you're not here, hence why it's impossible for me to simply throw you the key to this cell."

Alexius's dark eyes narrowed. "If you think that I'm going to be giving you information about my friends and allies so you can take it back to the Dark Lord, you're wrong."

"If I wanted to get that information out of you, I would, and there's nothing you could do to stop me," said Jayce, unable to resist antagonising the knight a bit. "But have no fear, I won't force you to betray your friends. That would hardly be fair."

Alexius eyed him dubiously. As if fair play was the last thing he expected from Jayce and didn't believe him for a moment when he spoke of fairness. "Then what do you propose?"

"The Dark Lord asked me to learn what you know about your forces and the Hero in particular, but he never made any specifications that it had to be truthful. After two days, spin me whatever tales you can come up with, just so long as they are believable."

"Why after two days?"

"Again, for believability's sake," Jayce explained. "Also, the more time they think I need with you, the more likely you'll be left alone by everyone but myself."

After a moment, Alexius shook his head and let out a sound that was something between a laugh and a groan. "And just how am I supposed to know I can even trust you?"

Irritation speared through Jayce, and it was all he could do to keep himself from reaching for his magic and using it to slam the knight's head against the wall.

"I'm not going to allow any second guessing, Sir Knight," Jayce snarled. "You were the one who offered to help me in the first place, and I am taking you up on that offer. Either you stick to your word or maybe I will decide to hand over my interrogation duties to General Detlas. I don't think there's anything you'll be able to say that will sway him from actually carrying it out."

Alexius stared hard at him with those black eyes of his. Until he closed them, and Jayce knew he had won this exchange.

"Fine," Alexius said like a man at the end of his rope. "I'll uphold my word. On my knight's honour."

"Good," said Jayce. Before he could say more, Alexius interrupted him.

"There is something else I'd like to ask of you in exchange for my help."

"What is it?"

"Can you at least unchain me?"

Jayce did, and the two of them finally got to discussing what it was he had come here to talk about in the first place.

"My father was a university professor, and his study was filled with the rare artefacts that he researched," Alexius told him. "Including a collar just like that one."

Jayce forced himself not to touch the collar in question. "Get to the point."

"I asked him about it one day. I thought it would be nice to wear. I was about seven or eight at the time. He told me why I couldn't, of course. He said that if I put it on, I'd never be able to get it off. Unless I had the key."

"If you're going to tell me that the key is all I need, then we are wasting our time," said Jayce. "I watched the Dark Lord destroy it right after he put the collar on me."

"I wasn't finished," Alexius said. "The key is only one way of taking off one of those collars. The other way is to disable its magic."

"And just how do you do that?"

"Not easily. You need a void crystal."

A void crystal. Why hadn't he ever thought of that before? *Probably because they're next to impossible to find,* he thought irritably. Void crystals were unassuming black stones that acted as magical inhibitors. No one knew what it was about them that rendered magic useless in their presence, but some years ago, the then king of Solière—who was a wizard himself—decreed that all such crystals be found and destroyed. Which is why void crystals were so scarce these days.

"I told you, it would not be easy," Alexius said, perhaps noticing the look on Jayce's face.

No. No, it certainly wasn't.

But that didn't mean it would be impossible.

Two days later, he went straight to the Dark Lord's apartments. Jayce found him sitting in the same wing-back chair by the tall windows, with a goblet of wine in his hand. It was almost as if he had not moved from the last time Jayce had seen him.

As his footsteps sounded across the floor, the Dark Lord turned to him with a mildly curious look on his face. "Yes?" he said in a drawl.

Standing straight, Jayce steeled himself for what he was about to say. "Our prisoner has told us the most interesting news."

The Hero and her army were planning on weaponizing void crystals, Jayce told the Dark Lord. The lie fell smoothly from his lips even though his heart hammered so hard in his chest that he almost feared the room would begin shaking with it.

The collar prevented him from disobeying the Dark Lord, yes. But Jayce had come to realise that on rare occasions, there were loopholes to be found. The Dark Lord had told him to report back to him the things Alexius had told Jayce about the Hero's forces. But he never said anything about Jayce telling Alexius what to say to him. He also never said that Jayce could not omit certain parts of his and the knight's conversations.

He said that the Hero's forces were scouring Solière, looking for as many void crystals as they could get their hands on, and use them to render his and the Dark Lord's magical capabilities useless by sewing the crystals into their armour and hammering them into their weapons.

"I see," said the Dark Lord. "That would be quite the problem. I think the solution would be to find these void crystals before they do and destroy them all."

"Actually, My Lord," Jayce said. "I had another idea."

"Oh?"

"Find the void crystals before they do, but instead of destroying them, why not take them for ourselves? After all, we know the Hero has wizards and sorcerers among her army. We could use the crystals to render their army incapable of using magic instead. Beat them at their own game."

Jayce could see how that idea pleased the Dark Lord by the burgeoning serpentine smile that showed a hint of pointed teeth and the spark that lit up in those yellow eyes.

"Yes. Yes, I like that plan. I like it very much." The Dark Lord rose from his seat. "Put the order out. Send out our agents and have them look for any sign of void crystals. If they cannot find any on our shores, tell them to set their sights to the other continents. And no void crystal is to enter the hands of the Hero's troops."

Jayce dipped his head in a deferential bow. "Yes, My Lord."

Only when he was out of the Dark Lord's rooms did he allow the smile to touch his face.

The hunt for the void crystals was as slow and arduous as Jayce had expected it to be. Still, it didn't make it any less frustrating when days turned into weeks and there was still no word about any void crystals having been found.

He tried not to let his annoyance show, although his master obviously felt no such compunction about his mounting frustrations.

"How do we know they haven't already gathered every speck of void crystals in Solière by now?" he had said while in the middle of a rage one night that had resulted in some splintered furniture and shattered glass.

"We can't be sure of that," Jayce said impassively. "We knew that void crystals are scarce, after all."

"Talk to the knight. Have him tell you the locations of their encampments. If need be, we'll storm their hideouts and take their void crystals for ourselves."

Jayce had had no choice but to obey. When he walked into

Alexius's dungeon cell to find the knight unchained—as Jayce had ordered him to be left—and picking dubiously at the gruel he'd been given for that night's meal, Jayce had said, without any preface, "I'm here to learn where your armies are hiding themselves."

Alexius had regarded him with the type of expression you might give someone when asked of your favourite food, before saying, "The hills at the Western Pass."

And Jayce had nodded and went back to report to the Dark Lord.

It was a dangerous game he was playing. He felt as if, at any moment, his bluff would be called. That the Dark Lord would see through the lies he was telling and make him pay accordingly.

But the Dark Lord didn't. He took Jayce's words for the truth he believed them to be. So sure of himself and the trust he had placed in Jayce. After all, why wouldn't he be? He had no reason to think that after all this time, Jayce was anything other than loyal. That the collar he'd put around Jayce's neck like one might do to an obedient hound, wouldn't prevent Jayce from acting in his own self-interest.

He'll see, thought Jayce, *just how wrong he is. About himself. And about me.*

It was early morning when the news came. About an attack on some of their forces near the Western Pass. Words such as "taken by surprise" and "heavy losses" were used to describe the incident.

"And the general?" Jayce had asked because he knew the squadron that was attacked had been led by Detlas.

"Alive, I believe," the soldier had told him.

Three days later, the soldier's words were confirmed when what little of the troop remained returned to the Dark Citadel, including Detlas.

Jayce knew when he had arrived because a servant, breathless from running, had come to find him as he was on his way to patrol the city.

"M-Master Grey, the general—the general has returned."

"I see. And you thought I needed to be informed of this

because?"

"He's gone to see the prisoner. S-Something about blaming him for the ambush."

"Fuck," was all Jayce said before he was practically flying back through the castle.

When he arrived in the dungeons it was to a commotion that ricocheted off the walls, which appeared to be coming from Detlas trying to get into Alexius's cell.

"General, please," he heard the dungeon keeper saying. "He's Grey's prisoner. We aren't to—"

"I don't give a fuck," Detlas barked. "I nearly lost my life out there and this bastard needs to answer for—"

"What's going on here?" Jayce stepped forward, making his presence known.

He peered through the open cell door and saw Alexius kneeling on the floor, hand pressed to a bleeding nose. So it appeared Detlas had gotten to him already.

Eyes narrowed, he said in a tone as cool as ice, "I thought I said no one was to lay their hands on the knight except for me?"

"You did say that, Master Grey," said the dungeon keeper. "But the Gen—"

Detlas pushed forward until he was standing directly in front of Jayce. The army general had yet to change out of his battle-worn armour or wipe much of the grime and blood from his person. His dark hair looked even more scraggly than usual, and his face was twisted into a furious grimace. Jayce couldn't help but think he looked like some deranged, wild animal in this state.

"That son of a bitch led me and my men into a trap," he snarled, one overly large finger pointing toward Alexius.

"And how exactly could he have done that, Detlas?" asked Jayce. "He's been locked in this cell for the past three weeks with no contact with anyone except for me."

"He knew our enemies would be there and—"

"Of course he did. That was why you and your men were sent to the Western Pass."

"We were told they'd be hiding out in the hills!" Fumed Detlas. "Not waiting to attack us in the forests a few miles south of there."

"With all your battle experience, General, I would have thought you'd know better than anyone that sometimes things don't go according to plan. Perhaps next time you ride out into a battle, you should remember to keep your wits about you."

The silence that followed was chilling. Jayce could practically feel the murderous intent rolling off of Detlas like waves of burning hot steam. He could see it in the other man's eyes, how much he wanted to strike out at Jayce in that moment.

Let him try.

But the moment passed and with a loud grunt, Detlas shoved passed Jayce as he stalked out of the dungeons. His heavy footfalls were loud even as they grew more distant.

Jayce said to the dungeon keeper, "Out. I need to talk with our prisoner."

The man didn't even hesitate. No sooner had Jayce stepped into the cell, closing the door behind him, had the keeper left.

Jayce reached into one of his pockets and threw a cloth down to the floor at Alexius's knees. "Here," he said. "You look like you could use that."

Alexius took his hand away from his bloodied face so he could pick up the cloth and press it to his nose instead. "Thanks." His voice came out muffled from behind the cloth.

Jayce watched as the white fabric quickly became stained with red. He frowned. "Nothing's broken, is it?"

"No." After a beat or two of silence passed. "Why did you do that? Intervene like that for me?"

"What makes you think I did it for you?"

"Why else would you have done it?"

Jayce didn't respond.

Alexius took the cloth away from his nose. "I don't know what difference it would make to you. Whether the others torture me or

16

not."

"You're helping me regain my freedom," said Jayce simply.

"I'm not helping that much. All I did was tell you of a way you could get the collar off. You've done the rest."

"Still. If it weren't for you, I would still be just as hopeless about escaping this life as I've ever been. For that alone, I owe you."

Alexius was watching him with quizzical eyes. He'd removed the cloth from his face. "Part of me has been wondering whether I did the right thing in offering to help you. I wondered if maybe, even without the collar, you'd still be a tyrant. Someone I would still have to fight against. But I'm starting to think that maybe that's not true, is it?"

"Believe what you will," Jayce said. "I won't try to tell you otherwise."

"I don't think you need to. I've been told that I am an excellent judge of character."

"We'll see about that," Jayce murmured.

Either Alexius didn't hear what he had just said, or he'd opted to ignore it because he asked, "How is the search for the void crystals coming along?"

"It's going about as well as I might've expected it to. Meaning that we've yet to have found any."

"Ah. I'm sorry?" Alexius said it uncertainly, as if he wasn't sure whether that was the right response.

Jayce lifted a shoulder in a delicate shrug, trying to affect an uncaring calm that he didn't truly feel. "I only hope for your sake we find them soon. I'm not sure for how much longer my master will allow you to luxuriate down here."

"I wouldn't exactly call my current situation luxurious," Alexius grumbled.

Jayce took the opportunity to really study Alexius. He hadn't been given a change of clothes and was still dressed in the dirty and ragged garments he'd been wearing when Jayce first met him. His black curls were growing longer and tangled and the stubble along his face was beginning to grow long enough that it might be considered a beard now. Even in the poor lighting of the dungeons, Jayce could see the deep, dark circles beneath Alexius's eyes. Signs of sleepless nights.

He was right. This was hardly luxurious living, but compared to what the Dark Lord might have in store for him, it might as well be.

Jayce saw a discarded tray of grey-ish muck and mouldy bread in the corner.

"I'll see if I can't talk the dungeon keeper into providing some more . . . edible food for you, at least," he said, as he turned to leave.

Behind him, he heard Alexius say in a soft voice, "I told you, Grey. I'm an excellent judge of character."

That gave him pause. Something was behaving strangely in his chest and before Jayce could stop himself, he found himself saying, "My name, my *real* name, is Jayce."

He was gone before Alexius could say anything more.

Later on, Jayce was just getting ready to retire for the evening when another servant came to fetch him. For a moment he feared that he was about to be told that Detlas was once again trying to seek vengeance against Alexius, but instead of filling him with dread, what he was told kindled the hope that had been starting to fade.

"They've found them. The void crystals."

~

Of course, it took another four days before the void crystals were finally delivered to the Dark Citadel. Even though they were intended to be used as weapons against their enemies, the crystals still posed a threat to them as well. Especially to the Dark Lord and Jayce, two of the strongest sorcerers in the Citadel.

So they kept the crystals in an empty chamber in one of the lower levels of the castle. A room with thick, stone walls, that would hopefully keep their magic-nulling effects to a minimum.

However, that didn't stop Jayce from entering the chamber in the dead of night.

Guards were supposed to be posted on the door to the chamber around the clock, but when Jayce entered, the whole floor was completely empty. Having been the one in charge of assigning guards, Jayce had made sure there would be a brief window of time between when the last guards left and the new ones took up their posts, just for this very moment.

The room was windowless and bare. The torchlight from outside, seeping in from beneath the door, was his only source of visibility, and there were almost no furnishings to speak of. Except for a long table at the far end. Scattered across that table were black stones that varied in size. Some no bigger than pebbles, while the biggest ones were half the size of Jayce's head. Void crystals.

He felt it as soon as he had appeared inside this room, the almost suffocating quality to the air. But it wasn't his breath that was being stolen from him. It was his magic.

Curiously, Jayce tried lighting a flame in his palm, one of the simplest spells a sorcerer could perform, and found that he couldn't. Found that when he tried, sweat pricked along his temples and a brief spell of dizziness overcame him.

So this was the effect of void crystals on those who wielded magic.

Clearing the dregs of dizziness with a shake of his head, Jayce approached the table and selected one of the crystals that was arrayed before him.

He took up one that fit snuggly into the palm of his hand and was as jagged as cut glass. Its surface was also clear enough that he could see a pale reflection of himself, even with the low light in the room.

Pocketing the crystal, Jayce slipped back out and into the still empty corridor.

His heart pounded with anticipation the entire walk back to his rooms. His heartbeat only seemed to grow louder in his ears with each step he took.

When finally he made it to the privacy of his rooms, lit only by pale moonlight, he wasted no time in undoing his cloak and letting it crumple to the floor as he took long strides towards the mirror across from his bed.

He pulled the long locks of his silvery hair back from his shoulders so he could have an uninterrupted view of the collar. That hated collar. No matter how beautiful it looked with its intricate metal work and shimmering garnets inlaid in the silver, it turned Jayce's stomach each time he laid eyes on it. To him, it was purely a symbol of his enslavement. When he looked at it, he felt the painful helplessness and fear exactly as he had felt it when the collar had first locked around his neck all those years ago. Just a hideous reminder.

Jayce took the crystal out of his pocket and studied its sleek, sharp edges.

"How exactly am I supposed to use the crystal to get the collar off?" Jayce had asked of Alexius a few days ago.

"I'm honestly not entirely sure, but I think you're supposed to hold it to where the collar interlocks." He had stood in front of Jayce, unexpectedly close as he reached out to put a hand behind Jayce's neck. "Here," Alexius said as his fingers touched the notches at the back of the collar.

Jayce took a steadying breath that did little to calm his rapid heartbeat. *Here goes nothing.*

He brought the void crystal up, and the suffocating feeling intensified. His vision began to blur at the edges when he lifted the crystal to the back of his neck. Jayce ignored it, instead focusing on touching the crystal to where Alexius had pressed his fingers on that day.

Jayce wasn't sure what he had expected, but the sudden onslaught of electrifying pain had never crossed his mind.

Crying out, Jayce fell to his knees, but never took the crystal away from where he had it pressed against the collar.

A sharp ringing in his ears deafened him to all other noise, even to his own low groans. The pain resonated all throughout his body. Like bolts of fiery lightning striking inside of him, threatening to turn every bone and muscle to ash. He barely even felt the pain in his palm from where the jagged edges of the crystal cut into the flesh there.

Right when he thought it was about to become so unbearable he might pass out, he heard something clatter to the floor and the pain stopped.

The first thing Jayce noticed was a foreign feeling in his body.

A lightness on his neck.

He opened his eyes, which he had squeezed shut at some point, and they were drawn instantly to the jewelled, silver collar lying on the floor directly below his face.

His hand shot up and when Jayce touched his neck, all he felt there was bare skin, damp and slightly warm, as if something hot had been pressed against it.

He looked up to the mirror and sure enough, his neck was bare. Free of the collar. Only some scarring ringing around the base of his throat and beneath his jaw where the edges had bit in over the years to serve as proof that it had ever been there in the first place.

That was not the only drastic change Jayce saw in himself. His hair, though still long, was no longer the metallic colour of spun silver, but had instead turned a darker, blue-black colour that he now remembered was the colour it had been before the Dark Lord snapped the collar around his neck.

And the black markings on both of his cheekbones had disappeared as well. Leaving behind only pale, unblemished skin.

It was almost impossible to believe, even with the evidence of it staring him right in the face.

The collar was off.

It was *gone*.

He looked down at the void crystal still clutched in his bloodied palm, and he no longer felt that smothering feeling coming off it. It felt no different to holding an ordinary stone.

Jayce flung it across the room as hard as he could, and it skidded across the floors with a high ringing. He tried summoning his magic, tried casting a spell, any kind, but found that he could not. That it was as impossible as trying to see behind him without turning your head or trying to reach for an object without moving your hand.

His magic was gone, too. Not that Jayce felt any sort of loss because of it. He'd never asked for the magic. He would live without it.

Besides, it was a small price to pay to have his freedom back.

Free.

He was finally free.

Before the realisation could fully sink in, there was a tremendous roaring sound, followed by the shuddering of the walls and floor. Like the world was tearing apart. It took Jayce a moment to realise what exactly it was. An explosion.

And Jayce had been in enough battles to know what a sound like that meant.

We're under attack.

Chapter
Three

Jayce pushed open the glass doors and stepped out onto the balcony, into the frigid night air.

And saw that down below was chaos.

Enemy troops had breached the city walls and were fast closing in on the Citadel. The Dark Lord's forces had clearly been taken by surprise and were scrambling to hold off the attackers. The sounds of battle echoed through the air, shouting, and the ringing of steel. Jayce could even see spells being cast. Bright points of flashing light in the darkness. A huge fireball took out a handful of the soldiers on the Citadel's outer wall.

Was this it? he wondered. Was this the inevitable final battle they had spent years preparing for? The battle that would determine the fate of Solière once and for all?

If it is, Jayce thought, *I'm not going to be a part of it.*

The collar was off. He was not the Dark Lord's servant any longer, but Jayce also did not wish to risk giving up his life so soon after he had finally taken back his freedom.

Turning away from the raging battle below, Jayce stalked back inside.

Let this battle play out however it was meant to. His role in this war was over.

After spending much of his life living inside the walls of the Dark Citadel, Jayce had ample knowledge of its lesser used corridors and secret passageways. Which had never come in handy more so than at this moment.

The last thing Jayce needed was for one of the Dark Lord's soldiers to spot him, especially when his appearance was so changed and he was no longer wearing the collar. It would only lead to capture first, questions later. Even with the battle raging outside, Jayce had no doubt that the Dark Lord would not take kindly to his men allowing his pet to escape.

"Where is Grey?" he heard from a guard at one point while he was skulking through a shadowy alcove.

"I don't know. No one's seen him."

And no one will if I can help it.

Jayce was walking along the hidden walkway above the gallery on the third floor, when he spotted a couple of soldiers in their black armour rushing across the floor.

"The Hero is here," one of the men said. "She and the Dark Lord are fighting on top of the tower."

"Should we help?" said the other.

"The Dark Lord wants this fight to be just between the two of them. But I heard the general's gone to fetch that knight from the dungeons. Something about using him to distract the Hero—" And that was all Jayce heard before the soldiers were out of earshot.

Alexius. In his exhilaration at having the collar off, and his haste to escape the castle unnoticed, Jayce hadn't spared a thought to the knight.

He owed Alexius, he knew that much. Alexius had no reason to help him in the first place, and yet, it was because of him that Jayce now stood a freer man than he had ever been in a long time.

Gritting his teeth, Jayce hissed out a "*shit,*" and darted back the

24

way he came.

The hall that led to the dungeons was thankfully empty. By the time Jayce reached it, the foundations of the castle had begun to shudder at irregular intervals, and he wasn't sure if it was the battle between the Dark Lord's army and the Soliérans that was causing it or the fight that was happening in the tower between the Hero and the Dark Lord.

He was also in time to see General Detlas dragging a newly battered-looking Alexius out of the dungeons.

Jayce brandished his sword, the metallic sound ringing through the empty hall. "Drop him," he ordered the general.

Detlas took stock of Jayce standing before him. A deep frown on his brutish face before it cleared and gave way to bewilderment instead.

"Well, I'll be," said Detlas. "Is that you, Grey? Lost your master's collar, have you?"

"I said drop him."

Detlas's small eyes narrowed, making them appear even smaller. He looked from Jayce to the barely conscious Alexius he was gripping by the back of the shirt. Jayce could see blood staining the side of Alexius's face, from hairline to jaw. Had Detlas hit him? Is that why he seemed hardly lucid?

"Oh, I see," said Detlas with something like triumph. "All these weeks of conversing with our prisoner here, trying to get him to share important secrets, was all just a ruse, wasn't it? You've been in league with him this whole time. You've betrayed us, Grey."

"Don't make me repeat myself, Detlas," Jayce said calmly, his sword unwavering. "You've always been exceptionally good at following orders. Like an obedient pet dog, so why stop now?"

With a sound like an enraged bull, Detlas dropped Alexius to the floor, while also drawing his own sword and lunging across the floor to Jayce.

It was almost instinctual for Jayce to reach for his magic to help him fight off Detlas. But of course, he did not have his magic anymore. He had only the sword in his hand and his own physical capabilities at his disposal.

Jayce had seen Detlas fight before and knew that he was quick on his feet even for a man of his bulk. He also knew that Detlas favoured a brutal style of fighting. Jayce had once seen him crush a man's skull in with just the heel of his foot.

To survive in an exchange with Detlas, he was going to need to stay swift on his feet and out of close quarters.

They went back and forth up and down the hall, their swords ringing against each other. Jayce's back hit the wall. He managed to duck in time to avoid the strike Detlas aimed at his neck. Instead, Detlas's blade scored a line through the wall. Deep enough to loose chunks of stone onto the floor.

The booming sounds of the battle outside were muted to Jayce's ears thanks to his own fight going on here.

He did, however, have his surroundings to take advantage of. At one point, Jayce cut down a tapestry hung on the wall and watched it blanket Detlas for only a moment or two before it was sliced apart and Detlas emerged from the torn threads and fabric.

At one point, the back of Jayce's foot caught on one of the pieces of stone that had fallen earlier during the fight. He lost his balance and didn't get the chance to right himself before he fell backwards onto the floor.

Detlas was fast closing in on him, clearly not intending to waste the opportunity Jayce's misstep presented to him.

He wasn't going to have time to pick himself up. *Shit*, he was going to die, all because he hadn't been paying enough attention to his surroundings—

Detlas reeled back, letting out a strangled cry.

That was when Jayce noticed a pair of arms around Detlas's neck in a stranglehold.

Alexius. He'd managed to sneak up behind Detlas without even Jayce noticing him.

He wasn't able to maintain his hold on Detlas for long, though. The general tore Alexius off of him and tossed him to the side as if he were no more than a bothersome insect. Still, it gave Jayce all the time he needed to get back on his feet and an opening to drive his sword between the gaps in Detlas's armour, near his abdomen.

Detlas cried out and before Jayce even had a chance to pull back, he was viciously backhanded, knocking him back a few paces.

From his knees, Jayce watched Detlas pull out the sword from his body, blood spurting forth.

It was then that they heard the call go out from somewhere inside the walls.

"The Dark Lord is defeated. Lay down your arms now and you will be spared."

He's gone? Jayce knelt in stupefied silence. The idea that the Dark Lord had been defeated, that he was no more—that the war was now no more—it was almost too impossible to believe.

Detlas made a wounded sound, and it reminded Jayce that there was still a present danger he had to deal with.

Even wounded and continuing to leak blood onto the carpet, Detlas glowered at Jayce with baleful eyes. The hatred in his expression was so intense it almost caused Jayce a pulse of fear.

"You did this," Detlas said, baring his teeth in a snarl. "Mark my words, Grey. You won't get away with this. I will make you pay for betraying us this day."

With those words uttered, Detlas darted to the side, disappearing through the stairwell that was the hall's second exit.

Jayce made to go after him, until he remembered.

He swung his attention to where Alexius was lying crumpled on his front, not too far away.

"Alexius," said Jayce once he was at the knight's side. "Alexius, get up."

But he remained unresponsive. His eyes closed. Jayce pressed a finger to the side of Alexius's neck and was relieved to feel the steady beat beneath the skin.

That was when he heard sounds on the main stairs and turned to face a trio of Soliéran soldiers, in rose-gold armour and with ornate swords in hand, descending the steps.

"Halt," one of the soldiers ordered him. "Drop your weapons."

Jayce raised his hands with an unimpressed look. "I don't have any weapons on me."

"Sir Alexius!" Another of the soldiers cried out when they noticed Alexius lying unconscious beside Jayce. "What have you done to him?"

"Other than try to save him, not much." The soldiers clearly didn't recognise him as Grey, but the black clothing he wore still singled him out as a member of the Dark Lord's household.

"Liar," said the soldier. "How do you explain all th—"

"Enough," snapped the first soldier, who Jayce assumed was the superior. "You two, see to Sir Alexius. And you." This time she addressed Jayce. "You're going to allow us to take you into custody. If you try to run or resist, you'll find one of our swords through your heart. Is that clear?"

With a sigh of defeat, Jayce extended his hands to the soldiers, offering them his bare wrists. "Crystal."

Chapter
Four

They put him in the dungeons along with the few of the Dark Lord's forces who had chosen to surrender rather than go down fighting. Jayce couldn't be sure how long he was left down there for. With no natural light and no clocks, it was impossible to keep track of the time. But he was almost certain it had to have been a few days by now.

I suppose this must be how Alexius felt, he thought, staring up at the shadows dancing on the ceiling as he lay on his back. *Perhaps it's only justice that I suffer through it too, and maybe that's why he's left me down here.*

Of course, there was another possible reason for why he was left in the dungeons that he tried hard not to dwell on.

Jayce was at least thankful that he had been given his own cell, so he didn't have to concern himself with questions that would follow if the other prisoners figured out who he was.

When Jayce was next visited, it was not by a surly or timid foot soldier carrying a tray of water, hard bread, and bland soup. Instead, it was a face he recognised all too well.

"Joséphine," said Jayce.

The Hero—and now the Saviour—of Solière glared at him with

contempt from the other side of the barred door. It had been some months since they had last come face to face with each other, but Joséphine had not changed that much. She was still tall and broad in the shoulders and . . . well, every other part of her, really. Her skin was a deep brown, even darker than Alexius's, and riddled with scars from years of battling to rid Solière of the Dark Lord and his forces.

Her hair had grown longer since he last saw her. The dark braids now fell to her waist. In the poor dungeon lighting, they looked like black cords of rope against the grey of her cloak.

"Grey," she snarled.

That's not my name anymore, he almost said, before deciding to let it be. He was a little stunned she recognised him. No one else had seemed to, so far. "I'm surprised you didn't come here sooner. Surely the sight of me powerless and rotting in a dungeon would fill you with joy?"

"Believe it or not, I've had more important business to attend to."

"More important than me? I'm hurt."

"But I can't deny seeing you like this does bring me some joy." Joséphine sighed. "Too bad it has to come to an end."

With a frown, Jayce opened his mouth to demand what she meant by that, when someone else appeared at the barred door of his cell.

"All right," Alexius said to Joséphine, "I think you've spent enough time just standing here taunting him. Hurry up and get this door open."

"You're no fun, Alexius," Joséphine said, even as she produced a ring of keys, selected one and inserted it into the keyhole, twisting it around some until there was a metallic snap and the door opened.

Alexius stepped into the cell first. Coming to kneel in front of Jayce. He had taken the ring of keys from Joséphine and set about using the large, rusted key with the square head to unlock Jayce's shackles.

Alexius looked different now, Jayce observed. No longer was he dirty and dishevelled after spending weeks locked in the dungeons. He now looked clean and well-rested. His face was freshly shaven, his hair closely cropped at the back and sides but with a nest of tight black curls at the top. He'd switched out his blood-stained garments for a pristine, red tunic beneath a grey travelling cloak and dark breeches and boots.

It was the first time Jayce had seen him in a presentable state and he absently thought that if he had found Alexius attractive even after days on end spent in a dark and filthy dungeon, then it was nothing compared to the Alexius before him now.

The manacles fell away and Jayce rubbed at his wrists, not without some relief to finally be free of the chafing weight of them.

"We'll try to find you something to soothe that," Alexius said, indicating the red welts on Jayce's skin where the manacles had dug in.

"It's fine," said Jayce dismissively as he pushed himself to his feet. "I'm more concerned with what exactly is going on here?"

"What does it look like?" Joséphine said from where she lingered in the doorway. "We're freeing you."

Jayce waited for them to start laughing. To let him know that Joséphine was joking. But they didn't.

Instead, what Alexius said was, "I'm leaving for Étoisaint tonight, and I want you to come with me, Jayce."

This wasn't a jest. They were being serious. They were willing to let him walk freely out of this dungeon. Not only that, but Alexius was asking Jayce to travel with him to his hometown.

Jayce had been expecting this to end with his head in a guillotine, or worse, to be left to rot in this dank cell for the rest of his days.

Which was why he felt like he was having such difficulty trying to wrap his head around what Alexius and Joséphine were telling him now.

Alexius must have noticed his hesitation. "I told you I would help you take back your freedom. And I intend to keep my word. There's nothing here for you now, Jayce. I will not force you to come to Étoisaint with me. If you wish to make your own way, you can do so. But I suggest leaving the Citadel tonight, while the streets are empty enough you won't run the risk of running into anyone."

That's the first time I've heard him call me by my real name, Jayce thought, and then said, "But—I don't understand. Why are you doing this? You know who I am. You know what I've done."

"I know. But I also told you I'm an excellent judge of character. And I've come to truly believe that if it wasn't for that collar around your neck all these years, you would never have done all those things."

"You can't know that."

"Then tell me why you came back for me the other day?" demanded Alexius. "Why did you stop to save me from Detlas when you could have used the confusion of the battle to escape? Why did you spend weeks before then making sure no one else would lay a finger on me?"

Jayce did not answer him. Instead, he turned his attention to Joséphine. "And you? You would just let me go free from here? After everything I've done?"

Asking felt like poking a bear with a stick, and judging by the look she gave him, that bear was contemplating rearing up to club him with her mighty paws. However, once more, he was mistaken.

"Alexius explained everything to me," she told him. "About the collar. And while there are many things I don't think I can forgive you for, it would seem that you were just another victim of the Dark Lord."

"How do you know? How do you know I didn't enjoy every second of it?" There he went, poking the bear again.

This time Joséphine's gaze darkened, but that was all the reaction she showed. "I don't. And I do not trust you one bit. If it were up to me, your fate would be left up to the people whose lives you ruined. But I do trust Alexius and he seems convinced you have a good heart and should be given the chance to begin anew. Now, no more questions." She took the bundle and tossed it onto the floor at his feet. "We can't stand around here all night, but I doubt it will do you any good to go travelling through Solière dressed in the Dark Lord's colours."

Jayce picked up the bundle and discovered it was clothes. A hooded, grey cloak wrapped around a plain, white shirt, blue jacket with quarter inch sleeves and grey trousers and a pair of boots. Unassuming peasant's garb.

"Get changed quickly," Alexius told him. "We'll wait outside."

Once Alexius and Joséphine left the cell, Jayce began undressing. Switching out his black robes for the ones he had been given.

As he changed, he could hear Alexius and Joséphine conversing in the corridor.

"Come with us, Josie," Alexius was saying. "I'm sure you miss home as much as I do after all this time."

"I'm not going home, Alex," came Joséphine's voice. "Not for a long time, I think."

"What? But why? You may be the Saviour of Solière, but you are not her queen. You've already done your duty. You deserve to rest now."

"You're right. I do deserve rest. In fact, I'd say I deserve more than that. I deserve to live my life however I want. Which is why I'm leaving Solière, to travel the other continents."

There was a pause. "You're . . . leaving? For how long?"

"I don't know. For as long as I want to, I suppose? Oh, Alexius, don't look at me like that. For so many years now, I've been little more than Solière's Hero. Destined to fight the Dark Lord, even if it kills her. I did not know whether I would live this long, Alexius. I was prepared to die, but I lived. And now that it is done, now that the Dark Lord is gone and my home and my loved ones are safe, I want to start living life on my own terms. I want to have my own, non-life-threatening adventures."

"I understand," said Alexius, although Jayce didn't fail to hear the note of sadness in his tone. But surely Alexius would follow her. That he must desire to get away with his lover? Perhaps now he was unwilling to see Jayce to Étoisaint? Maybe he should tell Alexius that he was more than capable of finding his own way there.

Once Jayce was dressed, he stepped out of the cell to meet Alexius and Joséphine.

Signs of the battle that had been waged here only days ago were still evident in the streets of the city. Pathways were still littered with debris. Some buildings still had holes in their rooftops or were missing entire walls.

But Jayce also noticed signs of jubilation. Ribbons wrapped around streetlamps that made him think there might have been celebrations not that long ago. On one partially collapsed brick wall, someone had written in red paint *The Saviour of Solière was here* and on another wall was **FREEDOM**.

Jayce, Alexius, and Joséphine stuck to travelling down the back alleys where they were less likely to encounter anyone who might still be wandering the streets at this time of night.

Luckily, they were able to make it down to the stables near the city gates without being noticed by anyone.

Waiting for them in the stables were two horses, already saddled and bridled. One was a black gelding with a glossy coat, and the other a chestnut mare.

"Blackfire," Alexius said affectionately to the gelding, stepping forward to stroke its velvety nose. "I've missed you, boy. Did you miss me?"

The horse answered by trying to lip at his face, making Alexius laugh.

"A couple of soldiers brought him in just this morning," said Joséphine. "I thought it would make for a nice surprise for you."

"It is. Thank you."

Jayce stepped over to the mare, who showed no real interest in him, and began looking through the saddlebags at her side. In there, he found a waterskin, and some food. The horse was also carrying a bedroll and blanket.

"What do the people think happened to Grey?" he couldn't help but ask.

Alexius exchanged a look with Joséphine before she said, "We made the announcement yesterday that Grey had died in the battle along with his master."

"We thought it for the best that everyone thinks Grey is dead," Alexius added. "For obvious reasons."

Of course, Jayce thought. It wouldn't do to have people go on believing that Grey was still alive and out there somewhere. Too many people would want him found and brought to justice. Too many would want to seek revenge. Jayce would have had to spend the rest of his days looking over his shoulder.

But Jayce supposed it was also the truth. Grey had died on the night of the battle. He'd ceased to exist the moment the collar came off of Jayce's neck.

He and Alexius mounted their horses.

"Goodbye, Alexius," said Joséphine. "And have a safe journey home."

"And to you," Alexius returned with a warm smile. "Take care of yourself, Josie. And try not to find any new trouble to get into on your travels."

"Don't worry about me. I'm sure Ollia will keep me in check."

That was the last they spoke to each other before Alexius urged Blackfire forward. With Jayce following behind, they left the stables and moved onto the road.

Hm, I would have expected them to have a more . . . intimate farewell than that, Jayce thought, turning to watch as the figure of Joséphine standing at the stables grew smaller and smaller.

They passed through without any disturbance from the guards. In fact, there were no guards to be seen, as far as Jayce could tell.

"Well, thanks to you, I had the idea to change the posting schedules a little bit," Alexius explained when Jayce questioned him about it. "To give us some time to leave unnoticed. But it's nothing to worry about, new guards should be taking up their posts soon enough. Joséphine will make sure of it."

Before long, they were out on the open road, beneath the starlit sky and among the desolate fields that Jayce was sure, given time, would be as green and fertile as they once were. It was hard to picture it now, but there was no doubt that one day this land would be given over to growing fruits and vegetables, pastures for grazing cattle and sheep. Maybe even small villages would begin to spring up.

Very soon, Jayce imagined that this place that had for so long been a place of misery and dead and dying things, would be a place for life.

It would find new life, just as Jayce would.

"Do you—Do you feel sad?" Alexius asked after a while, sounding hesitant. "To be leaving after all this time?"

Jayce looked back at the Citadel that was now little more than a black, pointed silhouette against the starry sky.

The Dark Citadel had been his prison for so many years. The place he always had to return to, no matter how desperately he wanted to run as far away from it as he could and never return.

And now, finally, here he was. Leaving, watching it diminish into the distance, knowing that he would never have to set foot back there for as long as he lived.

With a quirk of his lips, Jayce answered, "Not in the slightest."

Chapter
Five

"It's a long trip back to Étoisaint," Alexius told him on the morning of their first day of travel. "A three-week journey, at least."

"Is there any chance there's a faster way to get there?"

Alexius snorted. "Not unless you wish to cut through the Bleak Marshes. And I don't know about you, but I'd sooner live the rest of my life in that dungeon than set foot in the Marshes."

Funnily enough, the skies opened up that evening, releasing a deluge of rain that turned the roads thick with mud as well as snow and had the hood of Jayce's cloak dripping water into his face. The only place close enough for them to take shelter for the night was a copse of trees by the side of the road. And it also happened to be some distance from the Bleak Marshes, which was like a long, dark shape on the horizon.

When Jayce suggested that was where they spend the night, Alexius looked horrified. "You want us to sleep here? Near the Bleak Marshes?"

"We're hardly near it. It's a good few yards away. I doubt any kelpies or crones are going to come wandering this far out."

Alexius still looked hesitant, so Jayce said, "I guess the brave Sir

Alexius of Étoisaint is not so brave after all. In fact, he seems to be quite cowardly."

That got Alexius to swallow down his disinclinations, puff up his chest and lead Blackfire to the copse.

The trees didn't shield them completely from the rain, but it was still better than riding out in the brunt of it. They tied their horses to one of the trees and ate a quick meal of dried meat and salted biscuits while they sat in the damp snow and mud.

"There's something I have been meaning to ask you," Jayce said as they ate.

"Hm?"

"The reason you offered to bring me back to Étoisaint with you. It's so that you can keep an eye on me, isn't it? Because if you're wrong about me, you don't want people to suffer the consequences of your bad judgement."

There was a prominent hesitation before Alexius answered. "I—Yes. You're right." He sounded almost ashamed to admit it. "I don't think I am wrong about you, Jayce. But . . . it's not a chance I want to take."

There was no more conversation after that.

Afterwards, Jayce decided to take up the first watch, because while he wouldn't admit it aloud, Alexius had been right to be concerned about being stranded in the middle of a lonely road at night. There was every chance they could be discovered by bandits or hungry wildlife that might think to try and make a meal out of their horses. Or of Jayce and Alexius.

And then, of course, there was the Bleak Marshes, much closer to them than Jayce would have preferred.

As if on cue, a bone-chilling wail sounded through the air. The horses shifted and snorted fretfully. Jayce stood up to go calm them.

"What was that?" he heard Alexius say from where he was sitting up in his bedroll.

"It sounded like a crone to me."

"A what?"

"A crone." Still calmly stroking the wide neck of his chestnut mare, he looked at Alexius from over his shoulder. "Haven't you ever seen one before?"

Even in the dark, he could see Alexius shaking his head. "Have you?"

"Yes."

"What do they look like?"

"They . . . they look like old women."

Alexius laughed, and, oddly enough, Jayce felt a flush of embarrassment.

"It's true," he said defensively. "They look like old women turned into monsters. And the colour of their skin looks like it belongs to a drowned corpse. Their eyes are milk white, and they have the worst smell about them. Which makes sense, I suppose. I read somewhere that they don't consume their kills until they're properly rotten."

"How charming." Alexius's tone suggested he found it anything but. "Are you certain none of them will wander over here?"

Jayce peered over at the Marshes, that looked like little more than a black expanse of earth in the distance. If they were still in the daylight hours, he'd feel more confident in saying no. However, with the night sky casting the world in shades of darkness, Jayce wasn't sure he could safely say whether the creatures would stay confined to their marshes.

Still, he didn't need Alexius fretting all night. "I'd say we're a safe enough distance away."

Alexius seemed satisfied enough with the answer, and after a moment or two, he lay back down, turned over, and went to sleep.

Meanwhile, Jayce went back to his watch.

He wasn't sure how much time had passed when he heard something approaching.

Believing it to be a bandit, a wild animal, or maybe even a creature from the Marshes, Jayce's hand went instantly to the sword resting on the ground at his side. Climbing slowly to his feet, he unsheathed the blade, holding it at the ready as he crept slowly towards the approaching figure.

It was only when Jayce reached the edge of the copse did he get a proper look at what was coming towards them.

Striding across the snowy field was a creature Jayce had only before read about, never actually seen with his own two eyes. A unicorn.

With a distinctive ivory horn upon its head that looked as long as Jayce's sword and just as sharp, the unicorn was covered in a coat of shaggy white fur that blended in with its snowy surroundings. It was about as tall as a large dog and looked like a goat. Especially with its pale-yellow eyes with horizontal pupils.

Unicorns had not been seen in Solière for many years now. He'd heard murmurings once before that it was because of the war. Unicorns were said to only thrive in peaceful areas and Jayce supposed a land ravaged by war for several years hardly made ideal living conditions for the creatures.

The unicorn came to stand only an arm's reach away from Jayce. It switched its long tail and stamped one cloven hoof against the ground. As if it were waiting for something.

Jayce looked at the sword still held in his hands, then back at the seemingly expectant unicorn, before carefully lowering the blade to the ground.

The unicorn tossed its head in approval, its white mane lifting off its long, arched neck.

Unicorns were notoriously reclusive animals, so much so that there were myths that they only appeared to those who were pure of heart, for only they were the ones unicorns deemed worthy. Sometimes the pure of heart in these tales were replaced by virgins, so Jayce wasn't sure how much stock he would put into them.

Still, it seemed somehow significant that a unicorn was standing before him.

Jayce got to his knees, so he was closer to eye level with the unicorn.

He wasn't sure what compelled him to do so, but tentatively, Jayce reached out a hand to the beast.

It extended its head to him, its breath warm against his skin as it wuffled at his hand. Jayce held perfectly still, worried that even the minutest movement might spook the unicorn and send it racing back to wherever it came from or cause it to stick him with its horn. Another thing Jayce knew about unicorns was that their horns weren't merely for show.

But the unicorn seemed to hold no wariness toward Jayce. Once it was done smelling his outstretched hand, it rubbed its muzzle into his palm. Even lipping at his thumb.

He and the unicorn stayed like that for a few breaths longer, until it pulled away, blinked its long-lashed eyes at him and with another switch of its tail, it wheeled around and began making its way back the way it had come.

Jayce watched it go until it was barely more than an indistinct shape in the distance.

When he finally rose to his feet, picking up his sword, he turned back towards their makeshift campsite, to find Alexius, awake and leaning against one of the trees.

He was watching Jayce with a well-pleased look. As if he had just been proven right about something.

Chapter
Six

It took them the better part of two weeks to leave behind the war-ravaged lands of Solière, and cross into the parts where the Dark Lord's war had barely scratched.

The difference was startling. There were no ruins here. No unmarked graves or dead land. Here everything was still flourishing—if still patched here and there with the late winter snows. Land was still fertile enough for cows and sheep to graze and farmers to tend to their crops. The roads weren't deserted and more than once Jayce and Alexius passed other travellers, all of whom offered them a wave or a tip of their hats.

For Jayce, it felt almost as if they had wandered into a different world. The feeling only intensified when they arrived in their first proper town. Voisaille was largely a farming town, made up of dirt roads, turned soft from recent snowfall, and buildings either made from plain brick and mortar or wood panelling and thatched rooftops.

Chickens fled out off the road as Jayce and Alexius made their way through. A goat bleated as it was led along by a young girl with a length of rope. The air was filled with the cacophony of many voices speaking and shouting all at once. The smells of mud and cow dung filled Jayce's nostrils.

Although Voisaille was clearly no town for the rich, no one here seemed to be doing it too hard, from what Jayce could see. He saw children laughing as they tried to make sculptures out of the muddy snow. Neighbours smiling and chatting with each other from across their fences. Two men walked out of the tavern with their arms around each other's shoulders, singing loudly and laughing even louder. He wondered if the war had even affected this small town at all.

They arrived at the inn, leaving their horses with the stable hand out front. Alexius dropped a gold coin into the youth's hand before they made their way inside.

It was somewhat cramped inside, with many tables and chairs filling the already small dining space. The windows were small and scarce, leaving it dark enough that candles had to be lit even though it was the middle of the day.

"Only room available is the one out back," the old shadeborn with grey skin and short horns told them when they inquired about lodging for the night. "Meanin' you'll have to sleep next to the pigpen."

"That's fine," said Alexius. "How much will it be?"

Jayce saw the shadeborn look at them consideringly, most likely taking in everything about them, from the make of their clothes to the well-crafted hilt of Alexius's sword at his hip and decided on the going rate right then and there. Jayce fought the urge to pull his hood over his face when the woman's eyes lingered on him.

"Seven gold."

If Alexius was bothered by the amount, he did not show it and handed over the coin dutifully.

Setting her broom aside, the shadeborn led them out the back and into a small yard, where a ginger cat lazed on an overturned box and pigs snorted and shuffled about in their pen. Beside which was a shack with a lopsided roof. Inside was little more than a small room with two narrow beds, a small hearth in the back wall, and a floor littered with straw.

"No latrines in here, so if ya have a need to relieve yourselves, you'll have to come into the main house. And dinner's served at six, unless ya have somewhere else to eat."

With those parting words, the old shadeborn left them to settle in.

"Charming," said Jayce, as he went to sit on one of the beds. It made an ominous creaking sound as he settled his weight upon it.

"It's only for one night," Alexius said with a shrug. "I thought it would be good to sleep under a roof again."

No sooner had the words left Alexius's mouth did a small pile of snow fall to the floor from a hole in the roof.

"We may have a roof, but I still wouldn't say our conditions have improved all that much."

"Must you be so dreary?"

"Must you be so cheery?"

With an exasperated sigh, Alexius unbuckled his sword belt and laid it flat on the other bed. "We're also running low on supplies," he pointed out. "I'm going to go into town and see what I can get. Do you want to come with me?"

Jayce knew that it was unlikely that anyone would recognise him, especially this far out, but he still felt uncomfortable at the thought of being out amongst so many people.

"I think I'll wait here," he said.

Alexius didn't prod him on it. Just accepted his response with a nod, dug out his coin purse and left, telling Jayce he'd be back in a little while.

Jayce was left alone in the rundown little room, the muffled sound of a pig squealing outside breaking the silence.

You're going to have to get used to being out and about among large groups of people, he told himself, lying on his back with his arms spread out on either side of him.

It was an irrational fear he was going to have to get over and soon. If he was going to follow through with making a new life for himself in Étoisaint, he couldn't spend his days avoiding people on the slim chance that they would recognise him as Grey, even without the collar or the markings or the distinctive silver hair.

Don't be a coward, Jayce.

He heard a tiny sound coming from the corner. When he sat up, he saw a black rat busying itself with some of the straw on the floor. It went still when it caught sight of Jayce's movement, regarded him for a moment before scurrying off and disappearing through a triangular hole in the wall.

Jayce stared at the spot where the rat had been for some time. *It's only for one night.*

Eventually, Jayce did decide to venture out of the shack. But he did not go far, only making his way into the inn's dining room where he ordered himself an ale and a lamb pie—neither of which were anything to write home about, but they silenced the low groaning of his stomach.

He ate alone at the counter, with his hood shrouding his face, even though the place was empty aside from himself and the shadeborn innkeeper, who was polishing dishes behind the counter. At least until the door opened, and a gnome walked in and took up the seat beside Jayce.

"Ophélie," the gnome said to the shadeborn, "One lager and some of that beef stew, if you got any."

"Been a while since I last saw ya, Lambert," said the shadeborn, pulling out a large tin mug. "You could at least start off with a proper hello."

The gnome replied with a sound not too dissimilar to a growling dog.

Ophélie had the gnome's lager ready in no time and set it on the bench in front of him. Lambert grabbed the mug and began drinking in long, desperate gulps.

Jayce heard the old woman let out a low whistle. "That scar there's a new one."

"Really?" Lambert's tone was unpleasant. "I hadn't noticed."

For the first time, Jayce looked over at the gnome. He was brown-skinned with long, curling black hair and a close-cropped beard. He wore a rough-spun travelling cloak and had a crossbow strapped to his back. The scar that the shadeborn spoke of was a nasty-looking diagonal slash that crossed over the bridge of his nose and came to a stop just below the corner of his right eye. The wound still looked red and fresh, and Jayce thought he could still see stitches holding it closed—it was hard to be sure in this poor lighting.

The gnome took notice of Jayce looking and offered him a crooked grin that Jayce imagined would have been painful on the wound.

"My mug was ugly even before this," he said. "So, it's no real loss. But a handsome young thing like you ought to be careful you don't go getting yourself too scratched up."

Too late for that. "An injury like that looks like it could have easily been a lethal one," said Jayce, with light interest. "How did you come by it?"

"I was travelling way back south of here." Lambert jabbed a thumb over his shoulder, indicating where south was.

"What in the Gods' names were you doing there, Lambert?" asked Ophélie, sounding like an exasperated mother.

"I'd planned on joining the fighting! But by the time I'd even made it halfway to the Dark Citadel, the armies were on their way home and there was word that the Dark Lord had been defeated and the war was finally over." The gnome took another hefty swig from his drink and slammed it back down. "The only fighting I saw was on my way back when I stumbled across some fuckers from the Dark Lord's army hiding out in the bush. Which is where I got this from." He pointed to his scar.

"I think this is the first time I've heard someone sound annoyed about the Dark Lord's demise and the end of the war," Jayce said.

"'Course I'm glad it's all over," Lambert huffed. "But I'm a selfish bugger and I'd only headed off to that battlefield for one reason. To get revenge on Grey for killing my sister."

It took all of Jayce's self-control not to react outwardly to the declaration. To keep the indifferent mask firmly in place. But the hand that was hidden beneath his cloak tightened into a trembling fist in his lap.

"Lambert." This time Ophélie's voice was laced with pity. "Revenge isn't going to bring her back."

"I know that," snapped Lambert. His eyes were shining now in the dim light. "But it would have done me good, anyway. My sister was—she was the best person I ever knew. She was kind and good and brave and she didn't deserve to die. *She didn't.*"

The gnome began to weep. His expression contorted in a way that looked as if he were in physical agony.

Because of Jayce.

While the old innkeeper rounded the counter to put a comforting arm around the gnome, Jayce got off his stool.

It felt wrong for him, of all people, to be around to witness this moment of suffering. Unnoticed to the gnome and the old woman, Jayce slipped out the back door.

~

When Alexius returned to their lodgings for the night, it was nearing sundown.

And Jayce was shearing at his hair with his dagger.

"What are you doing?" Alexius asked, paused in the doorway with an expression on his face that looked torn between astonishment, horror and . . . amusement.

"I am cutting my hair." Jayce sliced off another lock with the blade. "I'd think that would be obvious."

"But . . . why?"

"Because it's too troublesome the way it is now," Jayce said waspishly. "Because it could still lead someone to recognise me.

Because it's still just a reminder."

"All right, all right." Alexius's tone was placating. He set down the bag of new supplies on the bed. "Just hold on. You're going to make a mess of things sawing it off with a knife like that. I'll be right back, so leave your hair alone."

In the first few moments after Alexius left, Jayce seriously considered ignoring the knight's words and taking the dagger to some more of his hair. But some of the fire that had been coursing through him when he had first picked up the knife had already died down. So Jayce let the dagger slip from his hand and fall to the floor with a metallic clatter.

True to his word, Alexius returned not a long time later, and with a large, rusty pair of shears in his hand.

"Admittedly, I think these are sheep shears," Alexius conceded. "But I think they'll do. Now," he took a seat on the edge of the bed opposite Jayce and gave the shears an experimental snip. "If you please?"

That was how Jayce found himself sitting on the cold, hard floor, leaning against Alexius de Viccarri's shins while the knight cut his hair. The 'schnip' sound the shears made each time Alexius cut away some of Jayce's hair was the loudest thing in the room for a while.

"Is knowing how to cut hair an important skill for being a knight?" Jayce couldn't help but quip.

"Oh, yes," said Alexius. "It's a myth that soldiers are made into knights based on the heroic feats they perform in battle. Instead, it all comes down to how well we manage each other's hair and how well polished we keep our armour."

"Hm, that makes much more sense."

Jayce couldn't help but let his eyes fall closed. The motions of Alexius's fingers meticulously combing through his hair, sometimes brushing his scalp, as he selected a piece of it to trim, was blissfully soothing. He had half a mind to request that Alexius never stop and that they stay like this forever.

"Are you going to tell me why you suddenly decided you wanted to cut your hair?"

Jayce's eyes opened, and he forgot about all the pleasantness of having Alexius tend to his hair. Instead, he thought of the gnome, Lambert, crying over the death of his sister. He thought of a charred battlefield, and the few survivors making a valiant—if futile—final stand. It had been so easy to lift his hand and create a wall of fire to consume the dregs of the enemy forces. He could still see their faces, the looks of despair and agony right before the fire claimed them. One of them had been a gnome woman. Not dressed in soldier's armour, but in healer's whites. A life lost that didn't need to be. Lost by his hand.

The torrent of wind created by the fire had buffeted the long, silvery strands of hair into his face.

"No. I'd rather not talk about it right now."

Alexius did not prod him further and Jayce felt gratitude well up within him.

"Turn around and face me," said Alexius after a while.

Jayce did so and Alexius leaned forward, his face directly in front of Jayce's and . . . close. Even as Alexius got to work shortening the strands that fell around his face, Jayce found it difficult to concentrate on anything else besides how close Alexius was to him. The little crease between his eyebrows, which were drawn together in concentration, the piercing black of his eyes and his full lips, parted just enough to show a hint of his front teeth.

This felt dangerous, and yet it had nothing to do with the shears being held near his face.

"There," Alexius announced, setting the shears down. He brushed a lock of hair out of Jayce's eyes. "All done."

The touch was so unexpected and caring that Jayce found himself leaning away from it before he could stop himself—had he wanted to stop himself? Cheeks feeling oddly warm, he patted the shortened strands that fell over his forehead. "How can I be sure you haven't given me a ridiculous haircut?"

"Maybe you should have thought of that before you let me cut it."

Jayce shot him a glowering look.

"I'm teasing. You can take a look for yourself when you go take a bath, because honestly, you need it."

Jayce glowered harder.

A short while later, Jayce did find himself in the small room on the upper floor of the inn, with a tub full of steaming water, a bar of soap, and a couple of soft towels.

He let out a relieved sigh as he sank into the warm water, letting it soothe his travel weary muscles. As he began the task of washing off the grime that had accumulated on his skin over the last week and a half, Jayce caught sight of himself in the old mirror hung on the wall beside him.

Lifting a hand to wipe away the steam gathered on the glass, he examined his reflection. It was as startling a change as when he had removed the collar and the markings on his face and the silver of his hair had vanished.

If there had ever been a time when Jayce's hair was so short, he couldn't remember it. The longest strands now fell almost all the way down to the knob of his spine at the base of his neck.

He touched the pieces that still fell into his eyes some and, for a brief moment, he felt the ghost of Alexius's touch. Alexius's fingertips drifting lightly across his skin. Which led him to thinking of Alexius looking at him with those warm eyes like onyxes.

Of Alexius, with his face so close to Jayce's.

And of what could have happened if Jayce had decided to close that small distance that had been between them.

This is very dangerous, indeed.

Chapter Seven

"Tell me about yourself," Alexius said to Jayce on their third day of travel after leaving Voisaille.

They were travelling on a lonely road that cut through a forest of towering trees, many of their branches still bare. The sun glared down warmly on them from beneath a thin layer of grey cloud.

"What?" was all Jayce said. He and Alexius rode side by side on their ambling horses.

"It just occurred to me," he said, "that I really don't know much about you."

"Good."

"Oh hush. I'm not asking you to reveal your closest kept secrets. But we've known each other a reasonable amount of time now. I helped free you of that collar and I even gave you a rather decent haircut. I don't think it would hurt to share some things about each other."

"Share about each other?" said Jayce. "So you're going to participate in this as well?"

"Sure! What do you want to know about me? I'll tell you anything you want to know."

"Really? Will tell me how many people you've fucked?"

Alexius cleared his throat. "That's . . . a little bit—"

"Relax. I'm only joking." Jayce tipped his head up, looking to the sky as a pair of sparrows flitted past. He did owe Alexius a great deal after all the help he'd given Jayce. Sharing some knowledge of himself was the least she could do. "I grew up on an apple orchard."

"That sounds nice. Where abouts?"

"I'm not sure. I don't remember much from before the Dark Lord took me."

"Oh."

"I was twelve, I think. I'd gone to the market in Redvale with one of the workers at the orchard when the Dark Lord's army attacked. They killed the man I was with, and I thought they would kill me too, but then for some reason, the Dark Lord himself took an interest in me. He brought me back to the Citadel and started training me up to be his apprentice. However, I was hardly the most biddable student. I tried to escape at least twice. The first time, they whipped me bloody. I couldn't get out of bed for a week. The second time I remember, the Dark Lord tried altering my memory.

He thought that if he could make me forget about my past, I'd be more obedient. But it didn't quite go as planned. Memory spells are tricky, even for someone as powerful as he was. He didn't manage to completely erase my memory. But he did a close enough job."

Alexius said nothing. Jayce could practically feel the dour mood surrounding them like a heavy weight. So he tried moving onto a lighter topic.

"I never knew my father. I think—I think he passed when I was only a babe. So, it was only my mother and I. I don't remember much about her either. Only that her hair was like mine and she used to read to me before I went to sleep."

Alexius chuckled. "Was that the only way she could get you to sleep?"

Jayce found himself smiling at the idea of his younger self being so difficult. "Perhaps. I remember playing in the apple orchards.

Climbing the trees and picking the apples off their branches to eat. We had a dog too. A big brown thing. I don't remember if I had any friends, but I remember that dog was as good as."

"I always wanted a dog when I was a boy," Alexius said. "But my grandmother didn't like them. All we had was a green parrot, Adélard. Awful thing. I stuck my finger into his cage once and he bit me, and my grandmother told *me* off for frightening the damn beast."

"Well, you did say you were the one who to put your fingers into his cage."

Alexius gave him a betrayed look. "Et tu?"

"I'm wondering if maybe you were just jealous of this bird since it sounds like your grandmother was very fond of it?" asked Jayce.

"Ha. Fond is an understatement, she adored that bird. But it was understandable. Before I came along, Adélard was all she had. My grandfather died before I was even born, and her only son went to live halfway across Soliére. It makes me sad to think that she was left on her own in that great big house for so many years."

"You said that your father lived so far away but you also lived with your grandmother?"

"I was born in the Crown City," Alexius explained. "My father moved there to marry my mother, but after they both died in a house fire when I was nine years old, I was sent to Étoisaint to live with my grandmother."

"And you and your grandmother were close, then?"

"We were."

They continued talking throughout the day. And the next. Jayce learned that Alexius had joined the Étoisaint guard when he was fifteen and signed on to be a soldier in the war when he was eighteen. He was knighted at twenty years of age, making him one of the youngest in recorded history to be given the honour. It had come after he'd helped to foil an assassination attempt on the Queen, which had been instigated by the Dark Lord.

In turn, Jayce told Alexius that he loved books, but hadn't read a single one since he was eighteen, and he missed reading terribly.

When night began to fall and they found themselves sitting across from each other in front of a small fire, Jayce asked, "What was she like? Your grandmother?"

"She was a tough old bird. She had no patience for nonsense, and she was strict. Very strict," said Alexius, tearing into his piece of cooked meat with his teeth. "I remember some of my friends were even scared of her when we were children. Including Joséphine. But she was also incredibly kind, and I never had to doubt whether she loved me. She taught me how to play the piano, you know?"

"You play the piano?" Although, it shouldn't have come as much of a surprise to Jayce. He'd taken notice of Alexius's hands before; the long and slender fingers made him think they looked more like the hands of a musician rather than a knight.

"Not for some time now," Alexius continued. "It's a bit difficult to keep such pursuits when you're fighting in a war."

Jayce stayed silent. He knew Alexius didn't mean it as a jab against him, but it still felt like it was.

Fortunately, Alexius didn't seem to notice anything amiss with Jayce's silence. "I still remember the first time I heard her play," he said. "I might have been twelve or so. I thought it was . . . magical. It even brought tears to my eyes."

"Listening to your grandmother play the piano made you cry?"

"I found the melody to be quite moving," Alexius said defensively. "Right there and then, I wanted to learn how to play as beautifully as her. She was thrilled when I asked her to teach me. Her father, my great-grandfather was actually a famous pianist from across the L'Vac, so I think she was excited to be able to pass on the skill."

"Truly? Where from across the L'Vac was he from?" The L'Vac was what they called the stretch of the sea that separated Soliére from the other continents.

"Thelos I think?" Alexius replied.

Jayce let out a small incredulous breath. "Thelos was where I was born."

"Oh?" Alexius looked at him from across the fire with pleasant surprise.

"My mother and I travelled here when I was only small." Jayce remembered parts of the voyage hazily. He remembered boarding the cog boat that would take them to their new home in Soliére. It was a rainy day, and he'd been gripping his mother's hand tightly. His mother has hoisted him up onto her shoulders, so he had a perfect view of the sea and the breaching whales in the distance.

"What was it like in Thelos?" Alexius asked.

Jayce picked up a twig from the ground beside him and fed it into the dwindling fire. "I don't remember."

In the pause that followed, the crickets started up their singing. A high droning that was already beginning to make Jayce's ears ring. The light of the sun was fast fading and the glow from their fire was becoming more prominent in the growing dimness.

"What's it like?" Alexius's voice was soft when he spoke again. "To not remember so much about your past?"

Jayce's first thought was to refuse to answer the question. It simply felt far too personal. But when he looked at Alexius sitting across from him, there was something in the other man's face that made Jayce relent. That made him feel safe to share this much of himself with this person in particular.

"It is . . . maddening. I want to remember more of the time when— before I became Grey. I want to remember who my mother was, so that maybe I'll have a better chance of finding her someday." He looked down at the open palm of his hand. Pale skinned and dirty from where he'd had it pressed against the ground.

If he gazed long enough, he was sure he could see red on his hand too.

"I want more memories from the time when my hands weren't stained with blood."

They were silent for a while once more. Finally, Alexius stood to come and kneel beside Jayce. He eyed Alexius inquisitively, but the other man kept his eyes downcast, his expression not giving anything away.

Alexius reached for his hand and surprisingly enough, Jayce allowed him to take it. Alexius held his hand gently in his own larger one. The colour of their skin in complete contrast to one another. Jayce's was almost ghostly white in the dying light while Alexius's was the dark colour of the newly turned earth. Of the trunk of an oak tree. Of something alive.

Still holding onto Jayce's hand with his own, Alexius finally looked up at Jayce with his warm, dark eyes and smiled.

No words were exchanged. Because they didn't need to be.

Because sometimes, even small gestures were enough to warm the heart.

~

"Do you think you'll join Joséphine on her travels sometime soon?" Jayce asked one early afternoon while he and Alexius stopped to let their horses drink from a river.

"I don't imagine I will at all," said Alexius. "Why?"

"Now that the war is over, I thought you would want to spend these new peaceful times with your lover."

Alexius's head snapped up from where he had been busy readjusting Blackfire's saddle straps. "My—Joséphine isn't my lover."

Now it was Jayce's turn to look surprised. "In the Dark Citadel we all used to refer to you as the Hero's lover."

"Well, you all had it wrong. Joséphine and I haven't been romantically involved for a few years now. Actually, she's been courting a woman named Ollia for almost a year. I'm sure she would have joined Joséphine on her journey."

Hm. So Alexius wasn't the Hero's lover.

Jayce couldn't pinpoint why, but for some reason, the news left him feeling a little lighter.

Chapter
Eight

Jayce was familiar with night terrors. After all, he had seen and done, it would be foolish to think that they would not plague him. That the blood he had shed, the tortured howls and wails he had elicited and the wretched faces he had caused, wouldn't be there waiting for him as soon as he drifted into sleep.

To say that he was used to it was, perhaps, a bit of a stretch. Instead, it would be more apt to say that Jayce had come to expect the nightmares whenever he lay down to sleep. Expected to awake sometime during the night, gasping and shaking.

What he did not expect, however, was to be woken in the night by someone else's nightmares.

Jayce found himself lying on his bedroll in the clearing he and Alexius had settled down in for some sleep, their forested surroundings still shrouded in the dark. It took him a few sluggish moments to realise what it was that had pulled him so forcefully from his sleep, until he saw Alexius sitting up beside him. Bent over almost double with his head in his hands and a tremor in his silhouette.

Suddenly Jayce remembered that it was the sound of yelling and thrashing about that woke him.

"Alexius?" he mumbled drowsily, propping himself up onto his elbows.

He heard a hitch in Alexius's breath, which had been hard and shaky until now. Without answer, Alexius pushed himself to his feet and began making his way towards the edge of the clearing, where their horses were tied and sleeping on their feet.

"Alexius? Where are you going?"

Still no reply. But Jayce noticed that Alexius was already working on untying his gelding. As if he meant to ride off somewhere.

More awake and concerned now, Jayce stood and crossed over to where Alexius and the horses were.

He placed his hand on the other man's shoulder. "What is it? Where do you think you're going at this time of—"

"*Don't.*"

Jayce's hand was slapped away, and he was blinking in surprise at the wild-eyed expression on Alexius's face. An expression that was so foreign on his face, Jayce found it more than a little disconcerting.

"Don't touch me," Alexius said—panted. "Not now. Not you."

Jayce's eyebrows drew together. "Not me? What's that supposed to mean?"

Alexius had turned back to Blackfire, but he was not making any further moves to prepare him for a ride. Instead, he kept his hands on his flank.

"You . . . You've killed so many people."

The words were ground out. Slowly and roughly. Yet they hit Jayce as quick and sharp as a whip. Leaving behind a similar sting.

"Really?" Jayce sneered. "Have you only just realised this? And here I thought we'd already established the sordidness of my life. I suppose you really can't expect looks and brains in the same package."

Alexius turned to give him a dark look. "Watch your words, Jayce."

"Is that a threat?"

The horses were beginning to move around in agitation, whinnying and flaring their nostrils. Perhaps sensing the hostility brewing between their riders.

"No," said Alexius. "Just a warning. For I do not wish to hear such slights from you right now."

"And I do not wish to have the horrible deeds I was *forced* to carry out with my own hands, thrown into my face when I have done nothing to deserve it!" Jayce hissed.

The glare faded quickly from Alexius's face, replaced instead by a taken aback look mingled with an awful realisation.

Jayce's mare reared, neighing loudly, the sound like a crack through the night.

He had only enough time to grab her by the bridle, trying to calm her when the thundering sound of approaching hoofbeats reached his ears. Quickly followed by five riders on horseback, charging into the clearing.

Alexius did not even have the chance to dart over to their saddlebags to retrieve his sword before they were surrounded.

Jayce reached for the dagger he kept sheathed at his thigh, even while he slept. But before he could even consider which of the newcomers' throats he could aim it at, all five of the men on horseback had loaded crossbows trained on the two of them.

"Drop the knife," said one of the men, positioned to Jayce's left. "And I won't order my boys here to shoot you full of bolts."

Their panicked horses were blocking the only way they could try and flee. Alexius was without a weapon and Jayce was armed with one dagger that would only serve to take down one of these men before he and Alexius were brought down themselves.

Jayce dropped the dagger.

They had their wrists tied behind their backs and their legs bound at the ankles with thick, coarse rope. Jayce knew he would have welts on his skin again.

He and Alexius were left to sit at the base of a tree while the five men rummaged around through their belongings, looking for anything worth taking. They'd already rounded up Blackfire and

Jayce's mare for their own.

"This is your fault, you know," Alexius whispered to him.

"My fault?"

"If you hadn't been yelling at me, then maybe they wouldn't have heard us."

"Well, I might not have been yelling if you hadn't been acting like such an arse," Jayce hissed.

A pause. "I said I was sorry for that."

"No, you didn't."

Another pause. "I was about to."

"Your intended apology is not accepted," Jayce said spitefully

"Shame there ain't much here worth taking," the bearded man, whom Jayce assumed to be the leader, finally announced. "Other than a nice sword and some coin, these boys have jack shit."

One of the bandits, a young man with scraggly black hair mostly hidden beneath a dirty cap, was admiring Alexius's sword. "I'm sure their horses will fetch us a pretty price," he said.

"Well now, if you're satisfied, why not let us go and make off with our belongings already?" said Jayce.

The dwarf, with both his arms covered in tattoos, made a rude sound. "So you can find your way to the nearest town and send the local guard chasing after us?"

"Hardly. My companion and I would be grateful just to walk away with our lives. We can always find new horses and belongings."

Out of the corner of his eyes, Jayce noticed Alexius giving him a sharp look. He knew the knight most likely wasn't happy that Jayce was practically giving these bandits his blessing to rob them for all they were worth. *Well, too bad. I'd rather not have my throat slit over a few coins and some hard cheese.*

"Too bad your word ain't worth much, pretty boy," growled the dwarf.

"I say we just kill them both now," said another bandit with pock-marked cheeks. He was already reaching for the blade at his hip.

Surprisingly, it was the bearded bandit who came to their defence.

"Hey, now let's not be too hasty."

He knelt down in front of Jayce and examined him as if he were a piece of cloth the bandit was considering purchasing. "This one has quite a nice face. His eyes remind me of jewels." A lecherous grin unfolded on the man's face. "How would you prefer a new travelling companion?"

This was not the turn of events Jayce had been expecting. But now that it had presented itself, an idea formed quickly in his head.

Jayce allowed a coy smile to slip onto his face. "A travelling companion? Is that all I'd be?"

Clearly pleased with his tone, the bearded bandit leaned in closer to Jayce. But before he could say or do anything further, there was a low growl of warning from beside him.

"Do not come any closer."

Alexius was fixing the bearded bandit with such a dark expression that it sent a little shock through Jayce. He never thought he would see such a powerful glare on Alexius's normally kind face. He didn't think Alexius had even looked at him like that when they first met in the Citadel's dungeons.

"You sure he's your companion and not your lover?" The bearded bandit asked.

"Of course he's not," Jayce said, keeping his voice steady. "He's just a brute who isn't even my type."

"And what is your type, sweetheart?" He pressed in closer, his calloused hand coming up to cup Jayce's jaw.

Alexius jerked violently. "*I said don't come any closer.*"

The bandit was beginning to look rather annoyed now. To keep his attention from straying to Alexius, Jayce said, "Maybe somewhere more private would do?"

That certainly made the bearded bandit forget all about Alexius. His leer widened and, wordlessly, pulled out a hunting knife from his belt to saw through the bindings around Jayce's ankles.

"Aw, c'mon, Marv," moaned the scraggly-haired bandit. "Right now?"

"I'm sure the four of you can keep yourselves entertained." Once his legs were free, the bearded bandit helped Jayce to his feet and began herding him away from the clearing. "While I . . . entertain myself."

Alexius called out to him, but Jayce refused to look back as he and the bearded bandit walked deeper into the forest.

They walked until they were a good distance away from the others. And only once it felt like they were all alone, did they stop and Jayce was pressed up against one of the trees, the rough bark digging almost painfully into his still bound hands.

"No jealous lover to interrupt us here," said the bearded bandit.

Returning the man's smirk, Jayce said, "Then what are you waiting for?"

Trying to cut through the ropes around his own hands with the bandit's hunting knife was awkward and took longer than he would have liked, but eventually, the ropes fell away and Jayce took a brief moment to luxuriate in the feeling of having his hands free.

Stepping over the sprawled-out form of the bearded bandit, Jayce began making his way back towards the clearing.

As he did, he thought of exactly how he would get to Alexius and how they would make their escape. There were still four more bandits left to contend with and once again, Jayce was only armed with a knife—too preoccupied with slaking his lust, the bearded bandit had neglected to worry about bringing a sturdier weapon with him when going out alone.

If he could free Alexius without any of the other bandits knowing, then at least they could have the element of surprise on their side, if nothing else. And Alexius's large stature led Jayce to believe he could fare well against four bandits with only his fists if need be.

However, his ideas of subterfuge and a planned attack flew out the window when Jayce returned to the clearing to find that most of the horses were nowhere to be seen and all four bandits flat on their backs, littered around the place like discarded dolls. The only one still standing in the middle of it all was Alexius.

He was no longer bound by rope and instead held his sword in his hand, the blade now spattered with red. His quick breaths were visible as clouds in the air.

Well, this all turned out easier than I thought.

"The rope they used to tie my hands was worn and frail," Alexius explained to him sometime later. "I could feel it from the start. But it was only after you and that bandit left that I was finally able to work my hands free."

After regrouping, he and Alexius had left the clearing and the dead bandits—at least, Jayce assumed they had all been dead—behind. They had gathered their things, hopped up onto the only two horses that hadn't bolted, Blackfire and a friendly piebald, and rode through the forest until they came to a stream.

Alexius's arm had been cut up in his scuffle with the bandits and Jayce thought it best to tend to it while they could, lest it run the risk of an infection. So, they'd tied up their horses while he and Alexius sat by the streambed. Alexius with his ruined shirt off completely while Jayce wiped away the blood on his skin.

"Taking on four bandits all on your own is impressive." Jayce turned to squeeze out the bloodied piece of cloth he was using into the stream. "If a bit foolish, though. It would have been safer if you had just waited for me to return. Maybe you could have avoided this." He gestured to the diagonal wound that ran along Alexius's bicep.

The other man shrugged. "It's hardly the worst wound I've ever sustained. And I might have waited for you . . . only I wasn't sure I should've been waiting for you. Actually, I thought I was going to have to rescue you."

That made Jayce scowl. "What? You think now that my magic is gone, I'm some helpless weakling? I wouldn't have gone off alone if I thought I couldn't handle him."

"I did not know you were going to *handle* him," Alexius retorted.

"I wasn't even aware you had a plan. I thought that—"

Jayce scrutinised Alexius's face as his words cut off abruptly. The knight's eyes were averted, his teeth digging into his bottom lip. He looked shame-faced, and realisation hit Jayce like a bucket of ice water.

He let out a hollow laugh. "A killer, a weakling, and a whore. I'm thrilled you think so highly of me."

"Don't say that," Alexius said vehemently. He looked upset, although whether that was because Jayce had made assumptions about him or because Jayce had degraded himself, he could not tell. "Of course I don't think that of you. I thought you had found yourself in a difficult position, and I know sometimes we simply do what we must to survive in times like those. I didn't think you would really let him—that you wanted to—"

Alexius trailed off, and Jayce sighed. He wasn't in the mood to carry that line of conversation any further. "But you think I'm a killer," he said softly and plainly. "You said it yourself."

Alexius chewed at his bottom lip. "I . . . I shouldn't have said that. I was—some nights I have these . . . horrible dreams. I've been told that, after all the fighting and the death and destruction I've seen these last few years, it's normal that such things would stay with me. Although, that does not make them any easier to deal with. Occasionally, I even see these awful visions while I'm wide awake. All it might take is hearing a particular sound or someone uttering a single word and I'm back on the battlefield, surrounded by people dying or back to when I had to carry a man who just lost both of his legs, while he screamed in agony in my ear."

Jayce watched Alexius lift his free hand to touch a puckered scar on his abdomen. "Or I'm seventeen years old again, being run through with a blade and feeling more pain and terror than I ever have in my life."

He lapsed into silence again with a far off look in his eyes, and Jayce allowed it. Because he understood all that Alexius was saying. He understood those dreams. Understood when the memories became so vivid it felt as if he was reliving them all over again.

There was even something comforting about hearing Jayce's experiences mirrored in Alexius's. Jayce wanted to tell him so. He wanted to say, 'I understand' or 'Sometimes the memories of the things I've seen and done are too much for me too', but he couldn't bring himself to. Not yet.

"And tonight, you were in one of those dreams," Alexius said. "You were the one killing all those people and laughing about it. But I know it's still no excuse for the way I treated you."

"You weren't wrong, though." Now that it was no longer needed, Jayce tossed the filthy cloth into the stream and watched as the water carried it away. "I have killed many people. Maybe—Maybe I don't deserve this. This freedom. Maybe what I deserve is to rot in a dungeon for the rest of my life. Or to have my life taken away from me."

"No." Alexius's tone was sharp enough that it startled Jayce, and his expression was just as fierce. "Everything you've done up until now was not your fault. You didn't have a choice."

"It still doesn't change the fact that so many people died and suffered because of me."

"You're right," admitted Alexius solemnly. "It doesn't. But forfeiting your life for the atrocities you were forced to do won't change it either. If you feel like you need to atone for what you've done, then do something good with your life. Be the person you should have always been."

"And what makes you so confident that I'm any better a person without the collar around my neck?" Jayce knew he shouldn't be inspiring doubt in Alexius. It was simply that the knight was so . . . good. So trusting. Alexius had lived through the horrors of war as Jayce had, and yet he still seemed full of idealistic views. Jayce couldn't help but want to rattle them.

"I just know it," Alexius replied.

"That's a terrible answer."

Alexius only smiled and said, "Maybe."

That trusting nature of his will come back to bite him one day. Yet Jayce found that he desperately did not want to be the reason for that. He never wanted to see Alexius look at him with hurt or mistrust.

It surprised him how badly he never wanted that to happen. In fact, Jayce might even say it instilled a fissure of fear in him. He'd never felt this way about anyone before, and least of all about someone he had known for such a short time.

He felt an echo of what he had felt at the inn in Voisaille, when Alexius's face had been so close to his.

Pushing his knot of confused feelings aside, Jayce reached for Alexius's discarded shirt and began tearing at the hem.

"What are you doing?"

"Your wound needs to be dressed," Jayce explained, "and we don't have any bandages on hand."

"But that's my shirt." Alexius sounded surprisingly distressed about it.

Jayce started wrapping one of the cloth strips around Alexius's wounded arm. "You have another shirt."

"Unless you're planning to use that one as well."

"You've figured out my evil plan," Jayce deadpanned. "My intention was to have you go bare-chested for the rest of our journey, but it seems I have been foiled. Darn."

"If that's all you wanted, you could just ask, you know?" Alexius gave him a sly smile and a wink.

There was that feeling again.

Jayce tied the makeshift bandage into a firm knot. As he pulled his hands away, Alexius reached out to hold him gently by the wrists. "What about you?" he asked softly.

"Me?" queried Jayce, unable to take his eyes off of Alexius's fingers against his skin.

Those same fingers shifted to lightly brush against the raw, pinkish marks that braceleted his wrists, from where the ropes had rubbed harshly against his skin.

Jayce raised his eyebrows. "It's hardly more than a bit of irritated skin. Nothing to get concerned over."

And yet, that's just what Alexius looked when he turned his onyx eyes up to Jayce's face. He still hadn't released his light grip on Jayce's wrists. "But does it pain you?"

Jayce sucked in a breath. This was—he was not used to this. To someone showing such concern for him. And all because of such an insignificant injury. He'd been hurt far worse than this before and no one had ever batted an eye. They'd simply expected him to heal himself. And he had.

"But does it pain you?"

Jayce did not know how he could possibly hope to deal with this.

He slid his hands out of Alexius's grip. "I can hardly even feel it," he said, climbing to his feet. "Now come on, let's get moving."

"Get moving?" said Alexius. "But we should sleep. After all, it's still—"

His line of speech died as he realised that dawn had already broken over the treetops.

Chapter
Nine

They arrived in Étoisaint at the crack of dawn, on the first day of spring.

Jayce's first look at the town was from above a high hilltop.

"There it is," said Alexius proudly from where he sat beside Jayce on Blackfire. He gestured to the sprawling town nestled between the expanse of rolling hills and forests of winter-bare trees. From this distance, the houses and shops looked no bigger than a child's building blocks, clustered close together. Trails of smoke were already rising from a chimney here and there and Jayce could see the thin, silvery line of a waterway that snaked through the town.

"Étoisaint. My hometown."

"How long has it been since you were last here?" Jayce asked him.

A melancholy look cast shadows over the knight's face. "Too long," was all he said before he urged Blackfire forward.

They still had a bit of a way to go before they reached the town, yet with every step that brought them closer, Jayce felt his apprehension grow. Was the fairy tale Alexius had spun for him about being able to make a new start in life really waiting for him here? Would he truly be able to walk through the streets unrecognised? He supposed he already knew the answer to that question when he looked back on the towns they had passed through and the people they had encountered over the last month. Not once had he even come close to being recognised as anyone other than merely another face in the crowd. Still, he couldn't help himself from wondering if perhaps his luck was about to run out.

"So," Alexius began, breaking the silence that had lingered between them since the hilltop, "I was thinking we should prepare a story for you, in case anyone asks about who you are."

"A month of travel and you only suggest this now?" said Jayce.

"You never brought it up either."

Jayce had nothing to say to that.

Alexius quickly forged ahead with the topic. "I thought maybe we don't need to make everything about your past a complete lie."

"How so?"

"Well, if anyone asks, you were also a prisoner in the Dark Citadel, and the tortures you went through damaged your memory. You have very little recollection about your life before you were taken prisoner, which is why I invited you to come stay with me for the time being."

"So we'll just be telling people an altered version of the truth?"

"Exactly."

"Do you really suppose there will be that many who will want to know all about my life's story?" Jayce wondered.

"I'm not sure," Alexius said. "But I think my house staff are going to be curious about why I'm bringing a stranger to live with me after returning home from war. And I don't think it would do to keep your past a complete secret. That might just invite anyone curious enough to try digging for more information about you."

"That is a good point."

Alexius looked at him from over his shoulder, his mouth curling up at the corner. "Then do you find my cover story to your liking?"

After a moment's pause, Jayce replied with, "It's adequate."

One thing Jayce certainly hadn't been expecting as soon as they set foot in Étoisaint, was the sheer number of people lining the paved streets, and the burst of noise that erupted as soon as the people saw them. Or to be more accurate as soon as they saw Alexius.

The air was frigid, especially at such an early hour as this, snow still covered much of the ground and the rooftops of the closely packed buildings, and yet it seemed almost as if every single townsperson in Étoisaint had left the warmth of their beds to brave the cold and welcome Alexius home with exalted cheers and applause and roses thrown at his horse's hooves.

When Jayce looked to Alexius, he saw that beneath the smile he offered to the crowds lay carefully concealed astonishment. Clearly, he had been expecting this kind of reception about as much as Jayce had.

Aside from all the people, Jayce noticed that Étoisaint appeared to be a quaint and colourful town. The buildings they passed were all made from brick with gabled roofs. Some were complete with small gardens, with fruit trees and rosebushes. The streets were wide enough to allow for crowds on either side and still have ample room for Jayce and Alexius to walk through.

They crossed a bridge that arced over a still thawing canal and found themselves in a town square, which appeared to be filled with even more people. A mosaic made up the ground in the square. Although it was hard to tell what of, with all the people standing around, Jayce thought it looked like a large, white star. A bell tower with a sharply steepled roof stood in the centre of the square. Standing beneath it, flanked by two guards in armour, was a man dressed in expensive clothing with a ruff so high it cradled his jaw, and a head of thick, black curls that fell past his shoulders and a thin, black moustache that curled at the ends.

Jayce knew just by looking at him that this must be the Grand Duke of Étoisaint.

Jayce followed Alexius to stand before the duke, but while Alexius dismounted his horse, Jayce chose to remain in his saddle.

He watched as Alexius fell to one knee in front of the man. "Your

Grace," he said.

The duke smiled down on Alexius like a father might have smiled at his son. "Welcome home, Sir Alexius de Viccarri. Now rise, a hero such as yourself has no business kneeling to the likes of me."

Alexius did as he was bid and once he was on his feet, the duke clasped him on the shoulder with a hand adorned with many gold and bejewelled rings.

In a voice that carried across the square and perhaps beyond, the duke addressed the crowd, "One of our brave soldiers, the valiant and honoured knight, Sir Alexius, has finally come home."

More ecstatic cries filled the air. Jayce's mare bobbed her head and shifted back a step, clearly growing agitated with all the commotion.

"We received word that you set out from the Citadel about a month ago," the duke was saying to Alexius. "And again, yesterday morning, I heard you were seen passing through Numelle."

"Thank you so much for the warm reception, Your Grace," said Alexius.

"We also have a celebration planned in yours and our other returned soldiers' honour this evening. I do hope you will be joining us?"

"How could I possibly say no? But before then, I would very much like to return home. It's been a long time on the road, and I should like to get some rest as well as get my companion here settled."

"Your companion?" said the Grand Duke with a curious look at Jayce.

"Jayce Marken, Your Grace," said Jayce, using the last name he and Alexius had only come up with some moments before entering the town. "I shared a cell with Sir Alexius in the Dark Citadel, and he has offered me lodgings in his home until such a time as I can make my own way."

"Ah, I see. As kind-hearted as they come, Sir Alexius has always been. Welcome to Étoisaint, Monsieur Marken."

Jayce bowed his head as Alexius swung himself back up into Blackfire's saddle.

Alexius spared one last wave to the crowd before he led Jayce out of the town square.

The de Viccarri estate lay outside of the town, to the north-west. When Jayce questioned Alexius about why they'd even needed to walk through the town at all, he'd explained that cutting through town was quicker.

"Then it had nothing to do with you wanting to bask in that hero's welcome?" Jayce asked, partly teasing.

Alexius shot him a sour look. "Of course not. How was I even supposed to know the duke had arranged something like that?"

"I'm sure there were plenty of opportunities for you to send secret correspondence over the last few weeks while I wasn't aware."

"Oh, be quiet," Alexius huffed.

He looked so childishly irritated by Jayce's needling that Jayce couldn't help but laugh. When he next looked at Alexius, it was to see the other man staring at him with something like astonishment.

"What?"

"You smiled," Alexius said simply.

"So?"

"I've never seen you smile before."

Jayce snorted. "Of course you have."

"No." Alexius shook his head firmly. "I've seen you smirk and curl your lip in a way that means you think something is ridiculous. But I've never seen you smile genuinely before. Or laugh." His expression softened. "It looks nice on you."

The sun was out now in all its glory, bathing everything within reach in luminescent gold. Including Alexius. The sunlight even glinted in his eyes, highlighting the veins of silver in his black irises, like the veins in marble, as they rested tenderly on Jayce.

And he thinks I look nice when I smile. Has this man ever seen himself in a mirror?

They said nothing more to each other until they reached the de Viccarri estate. Alexius's home was just what you would expect of a noble family's residence; a **château** in the middle of a small patch of woodland that Jayce imagined would be covered in the greenest of grass and jewel-coloured wildflowers once the snow cleared.

The house itself stood at two storeys high and was made from grey stone slabs and an elegant mansard roof. A stone fountain, intricately carved to look like two wolves frolicking, stood in the centre of the front yard and was flanked by two wisteria trees.

Standing in front of the fountain, looking ready to greet them as soon as Jayce and Alexius walked through the open wrought-iron gates, were four people standing in a row. There was a squat woman of perhaps middle years, in a dress and apron with a red coat thrown over. A dark-skinned man in a servant's black and white attire, a gnome with a straw hat on his head and a tall woman with auburn hair pulled back into a severe knot that revealed a pair of elven ears.

She also looked as if she were moments away from shedding tears at the sight of Alexius, yet she remained perfectly composed. Her voice was prim and proper and only wobbled a barely noticeable amount as she said, "Welcome home, Master Alexius."

"Estelle," Alexius beamed.

As soon as he dismounted Blackfire, he was stepping forward to embrace the elf woman, whose eyes went wide before her face settled into a small smile.

"All right," she said, patting Alexius daintily on the back. "That's enough now. Or you are going to end up crushing all my old bones."

Alexius pulled away, a wide grin still firmly in place. "Gods, it's so good to see you. All of you," he said that last part to the other three that were gathered.

"It's so good to see you again, too, Sir Alexius," said the dark-skinned man.

"Working around here just hasn't been the same without you around," the gnome said.

"Not even my own children enjoy my food like you do," added

73

the older woman.

Estelle turned her keen brown eyes onto Jayce, who stood by his horse, a short distance behind Alexius. "And who might this be?"

"Ah, yes. Everyone," Alexius began, "This is Jayce Marken. He was a prisoner in the Dark Citadel, and . . . has lost much of his memory, so he will be staying with me for the time being." Next, he went about introducing the others to Jayce. "This is Estelle. She's been the housekeeper here even before I came to live here as a boy." He gestured to the gnome. "This is Guillaume. He tends to the gardens and Blackfire." Next was the woman. "Abby, our cook." Then the dark-skinned man. "And Félix, he keeps the house spick and span."

"A pleasure to meet you all," said Jayce, inclining his head respectfully. "I hope not to intrude here for too long."

"Nonsense," Estelle said briskly. "A guest of Alexius is no intruder. Félix and I will go and prepare one of the guest rooms at once."

With that said, they all made for the inside of the château—except for Guillaume, who took up the responsibility of leading the horses round to the stables.

The inside was made up of soaring ceilings and polished mahogany flooring. While Abby made straight for the kitchens to whip them up a nice meal and Estelle and Félix saw to preparing Jayce a room, Alexius took it upon himself to give Jayce a quick tour of the house.

First, he showed Jayce the dining room, which was connected to the kitchens. The walls were papered with red patterned wallpaper. A large round table, draped in white lace cloth took up the centre of the room. Next was the billiard room—Alexius offered to teach Jayce how to play at some point. The study, which had once belonged to Alexius's grandmother. And lastly, an expansive drawing room, with soft yellow walls that only added to the brightness that flooded in thanks to the three tall windows overlooking the gardens on the wall opposite the entryway.

74

An ornate fireplace was embedded in the east-facing wall and above it, in a large frame of lacquered wood, was a painted portrait of a regal-looking woman with mahogany brown skin and thick, black hair pulled into a pile adorned with pearls atop her head. She had a proud tilt to her chin, and her dark-eyed gaze was imperious. She was instantly familiar to Jayce.

"This was your grandmother?" he asked, gesturing to the portrait.

"Yes," said Alexius. He was standing beside Jayce in front of the fireplace. "That was her about ten years ago."

"You look like her."

With a wistful smile, Alexius answered, "So I've been told."

"You never did tell me what happened to her," Jayce said with barely concealed hesitancy.

"She caught ill one winter and couldn't recover from it."

"I'm sorry."

"Don't be. She lived a full life, and I was told she did not suffer. I only wish I could have been with her when she passed."

"Where were you?" asked Jayce.

"Helping Joséphine find the Sorrow Blade in the Mountain of the Mists."

"Ah, I remember that," said Jayce. "I was supposed to go after you, but by the time I arrived you'd already taken the Blade and done quite the number on the basilisc."

"Believe me, he did quite the number on us, too. Come on," Alexius said. "I still need to show you the rest of the house."

There wasn't terribly much to see upstairs. There were the bedrooms, including Alexius's, which was down the very end of the hall, across from the room that had been his grandmother's. A bathroom, a small lounge room and a piano room.

They finished up their tour in the room Jayce would be staying in, just as Estelle and Félix had finished up preparing. It was a modest sized room, with a colour theme of green; green walls, a moss green rug, green velvet curtains and an emerald green cover with a leaf pattern on the bed.

"You heard the duke say there would be a celebration this evening," Alexius said once they were alone in the room together. "Would you like to come with me?"

Jayce was standing by the window, looking out at the gardens, full of flowers bushes and fruit trees that would be preparing to flower. From here he could even see the stables, where Guillaume appeared to be finishing up with his tending of the horses.

"No," he said, after a moment. "I think I'll stay here tonight."

"It could be a good opportunity to get to know the town a bit better," suggested Alexius. "Maybe meet some of the people."

"I don't—I don't feel ready for that just yet. Tomorrow maybe, but I would really prefer to stay away from such celebrations for tonight."

"All right. I understand."

Jayce looked over to where Alexius was still standing, with his arms folded by the doorway. "I'm not saying that so you'll feel obligated to stay with me, you know? I'll be just fine here on my own. Unless you're concerned that I might abscond with a few of the valuables I've seen around this place?"

Alexius let out a breath of vexation. "Will you stop that?"

Jayce tipped his head to the side. "Stop what?"

"Stop insinuating that I think of you as someone untrustworthy."

"I thought you did," Jayce muttered. "Isn't that why I'm here, after all?"

"No," said Alexius seriously. "I've made up my mind. The only reason I want you here is so you have a place to stay. But if you want to leave, I won't stop you. And don't think I've forgotten how you fought for me at the Citadel. Or how you had plenty of opportunities to double cross me over the past few weeks on the road, but you never did."

Instead of replying, Jayce returned his gaze to the view outside.

At least until Alexius came to stand in front of him, placing his hands on Jayce's shoulders.

"You're a good person," Alexius told him for what felt like the hundredth time. "And I'm sure as time goes on, you'll only affirm that belief."

"No pressure or anything," Jayce said wryly.

"Don't think of it as me pressuring you. Just think of it as some gentle encouragement."

Alexius winked and, ignoring the odd fluttering it caused in his stomach, Jayce said, "Fine. I'll do my best to prove you right."

And he meant it. If it was for Alexius, Jayce thought he would do just about anything.

Later, they bathed—separately, of course—and then they ate a sumptuous meal prepared by the cook, Abby, who seemed to have made it her new mission to feed Jayce as much as possible. "Your bones could do with some more meat on them," she told him while serving him a third helping of lemon tart.

After that, Jayce retreated to his room where he fell onto the bed and promptly fell asleep. A month on the road without a comfortable bed to fall into every night meant that he could not resist the temptation of slumber as soon as he felt the warm softness beneath his body. When he woke up some hours later, the sky was beginning to darken with impending nightfall and the house was empty except for himself and the elf, Estelle.

They spoke for some time in the kitchens over a plate of warm bread and meat that Abby had left for them. Jayce learned that Estelle had come into the employ of Madame de Viccarri when she was only nineteen, not long before Alexius had come to live under his grandmother's care.

"Alexius didn't ask you to stay here and keep an eye on me, did he?" he'd asked her.

"No. I simply have no taste for large parties. Unless, of course, I am the one who organised it." Estelle eyed him curiously. "Why? Should I be keeping an eye on you?"

"Alexius doesn't seem to think so."

"That boy has always been an excellent judge of character. If he thinks you're a good sort, then I trust his judgement. Also, you seem like a nice enough young man to me."

With nothing else to do after that, Jayce retired to bed again. When he woke up in the early hours of the morning, it was with the vague memory of Alexius appearing in his dreams. He couldn't remember what he had been dreaming about, nor why Alexius had been there. He only had the memory of Alexius's face, dimpled with a smile and looking down on him.

Jayce had the feeling it had been a rare, pleasant dream.

After lounging around in bed for a little while longer, Jayce finally decided to get up and get ready for the day—even though he had no idea what exactly he would be spending the day doing.

Making his way down the hall, towards the bathroom, he was brought up short when the door swung open to emit a giggling young woman with damp, dark hair and clad only in her small clothes.

It took a moment for the woman to register Jayce was standing there and that she was showing off quite an indecent amount of her bare skin to him. The giggles turned into a squeak and the woman hurriedly covered as much of herself as she could with the towel she was carrying.

Jayce blinked.

"I-I'm so sorry," she stammered. "I didn't realise there was anyone else up here."

Jayce was saved from answering by the arrival of Alexius, also coming out of the bathroom, and as similarly underdressed as the woman. He had a towel wrapped around his waist, but the rest of him, deep brown skin, shining from the steam of the bathroom, stretched over curved muscles that reminded Jayce of a statue carved by masterful hands, was gloriously bare.

He suddenly found it difficult to put his eyes anywhere else.

"Jayce, good morning," Alexius said with a bashful little smile. "We, uh . . . didn't wake you, did we?"

We.

Jayce thanked the Gods that he could speak truthfully when he answered with, "No. I didn't hear a sound."

"Good, that's good. Are you heading down to breakfast? Katrina and I will join you in a little while."

The woman—Katrina—gave him a little smile and a wave. "It was nice meeting you," she said before Alexius put a hand on her waist and the two of them turned away from Jayce and headed back to Alexius's room.

Jayce stayed rooted to the spot for a while, feeling oddly stupefied and . . . something else.

Something unpleasant and roiling in his chest. He thought of how Alexius and Katrina had exited the bathroom together, wearing very little. How obvious it was that she had spent the night and what it was they had most likely spent the night doing. He thought of Alexius's hand on her waist, guiding her back to his bedroom.

Envy.

That was what Jayce was feeling, and the revelation came to him with some amount of shock.

He was envious of the woman, Katrina. Of how close she had been to Alexius just now. He didn't know whether Alexius's feelings for her were simply lust or something more, but regardless, Jayce felt a wellspring of jealousy knowing that she was the one Alexius had chosen to gift with those kinds of affections.

Gods, Jayce thought, not without some agony as his second revelation of the morning hit him. *I'm falling in love with Alexius, aren't I?*

Chapter
Ten

It didn't take long for Jayce to grow accustomed to daily life in Étoisaint. And more specifically, life in the de Viccarri household.

Abby, the cook, arrived early in the mornings to prepare meals that never failed to make Jayce's tastebuds sing. Estelle could also typically be found around the house, making sure everything was running smoothly and that all of Alexius's—and Jayce's, as well— needs were met. Guillaume and Félix only worked every two or three days.

After a few days off, Alexius took up simple town guard duties. He'd even had brand new armour given to him. Sleek metal the colour of rose-gold, complete with a crimson cape.

There had been no more sightings of Katrina since Jayce's first morning there, which led him to believe that she had simply been a casual dalliance—he tried not to feel too relieved about that.

"I was thinking," Alexius said to him one morning over breakfast. "You told me you enjoy books."

"I'm flattered you remembered," Jayce said before taking a bite of his toasted bread, drizzled with syrup and sprinkled with cinnamon and sugar.

Alexius continued as if he hadn't heard Jayce's wisecrack. "I have an old friend in town who owns a bookstore. Perhaps I could take you there today and we could see if they'll offer you a job?"

That gave Jayce pause. "A job?"

"Well, yes. Although, if you think it's too soon and would prefer to get more settled in first—"

"No," Jayce interrupted. "No, we'll go today. Besides, the sooner I find some employment, the sooner I can find my own lodgings and stop intruding here."

He'd meant it as a joke, but Alexius looked at him with something akin to hurt. Like a kicked puppy. Jayce's heart couldn't take it.

"You're not intruding," Alexius told him firmly. "And I hope you don't think I'm only offering to find you a job so I can get rid of you. I like having you here."

Gods, must he be so earnest? Jayce hummed in response and took another bite of his toast. Trying to ignore the way Alexius's admission sent his heart thumping faster.

~

Tails and Tomes was a modest-sized building on the corner of Ebony Street in Étoisaint, right across from the canal. It had a blue-shingled roof and a blue-painted front door and was squished in between two other, larger buildings. Both the front windows were nearly impossible to see through, thanks to the piles of books that were stacked haphazardly in front of the glass. The name of the shop hung on a wooden sign right above the door in faded curling letters.

Tails *and* Tomes? Jayce thought, scrutinising the sign as he and Alexius stepped up to the front door. *Shouldn't it be spelled as Tales?*

Alexius pushed the door open, and the tinkling of a bell sounded overhead as they stepped inside.

The inside of the shop was actually much larger than it appeared to be on the outside. It might have even appeared larger still had it not been cluttered with more books than Jayce had ever seen in one place before. The walls were lined with bookcases of different shapes and sizes, all overflowing with different kinds of books. Some were thick tomes bound in old, cracked leather with spines the length of Jayce's forearm. Others were smaller, their pages not even yellowed.

While some of these books were fitted into shelves, there were also quite a few of them stacked on the floor in teetering piles taller than even Alexius. Jayce tried not to linger near those piles, lest they chose that moment to fall and crush him.

The parts of the walls that weren't covered by bookcases were taken up instead by maps of Solière and the other continents, paintings of landscapes and armoured knights battling giant, fire-breathing drakes. There was even an oil painting of a fruit platter.

Jayce also noticed a stuffed white cat sitting atop one of the shelves. Only, no, that wasn't a stuffed cat, he quickly realised when it turned its fluffy head to regard him with half-lidded yellow eyes before leaping down from its perch.

"Hello, Fable," Alexius said warmly to the cat as it came to sit in front of them, purring loudly when Alexius bent to scratch it under the chin. "Is Iris around?"

Just then, there was a loud noise like many somethings falling, and a shouted expletive from somewhere up ahead.

"Looks like we found them," Alexius said wryly before taking off in the direction the commotion had come from.

Jayce followed. They turned a corner at the end of one of the bookcases and were greeted to the sight of a pile of books that looked to have fallen to the floor and a toppled-over ladder. Standing in the middle of it all was an orc. Distinguishable by their green skin and the nubs of tusks protruding from their lower lip. But unlike all of the other orcs Jayce had seen over the years, this one was shorter—about the same height as Jayce, maybe—and with a much lankier build, as opposed to the seven-foot, brawny specimens Jayce had encountered before.

He saw they also had black hair cut short and large spectacles that currently sat crookedly on their nose.

"Everything all right here, Iris?" asked Alexius, taking in the chaos.

The orc—Iris—turned to him with a huff of exasperation. "Oh yes, perfectly. If you think almost breaking my neck while trying to stack some new books is *all right*, then yes."

"Perhaps stocking your shelves wouldn't be so perilous if you hired someone else to work here?"

"We've been over this before, Alexius." Iris began gathering up the fallen books around them. "That is not going to happen."

Wait. What? Jayce thought, perplexed. So they weren't looking to hire anyone? Then why in the Gods' names had Alexius brought him here?

"Now, if you'll excuse me I—" With all the books now gathered safely in their arms, Iris straightened and seemed to take notice of Jayce for the first time. "Oh. Hello there. I'm sorry I did not notice you."

"Iris, this is Jayce," Alexius explained. "I met him at the Citadel, and he's staying with me for a while. Jayce, this is Iris. An old friend and the owner of this shop."

"It's a pleasure to meet you, Iris," Jayce said, perhaps a bit too formally.

"Likewise. And not to sound rude, but why has Alexius brought you to my shop?"

Alexius didn't even bother to beat around the bush. "Because I want you to take him on as your assistant."

"Not going to happen," Iris snapped, pushing past the two of them with their armful of books.

"Oh, come on, Iris," Alexius practically begged as he followed after them, with Jayce being unable to do anything but trail behind.

"I have told you before. I don't need any assistants."

"But he needs a job."

"Then try inquiring at the tavern. Or go see if anyone needs another farmhand."

"But I thought working here would be perfect for him because he loves books. Isn't that right, Jayce?"

"Ah, yes. I do. Love books, that is."

Iris paused to squint at him from over their shoulder. "That sounded suspiciously like a lie."

"I know," he admitted. "But I promise I really do enjoy reading."

"If you say so."

"So, does that mean you'll hire him?" Alexius's voice was hopeful.

"No." The statement felt punctuated as Iris set the book stack down on the wooden front counter with a heavy *thwump*. Jayce noticed a faint plume of dust go up into the air.

"Please, Iris. Consider it a favour to a dear friend?"

Iris let out a long-winded sigh. "Why do you want him to work here so badly? Étoisaint is a big town. There are plenty of establishments that would be happy to take on a new worker."

Jayce's attention wandered away from the conversation when he felt something bump into his leg. Peering down, he saw the white cat from earlier, Fable, twining its body between his legs, purring loudly enough for Jayce to hear.

Before now, Jayce had only ever seen cats from a distance. Usually strays that loitered around the streets of the Dark Citadel and fled before you even had a chance to get close. If he had ever gotten the chance to interact with one before he had been taken in by the Dark Lord, he could not remember it.

Tentatively, he knelt down and held out a hand to the creature, allowing it to sniff him. Its small, pink nose was cool and moist against his skin. Fable let out a mewl and rubbed its head quite aggressively against Jayce's hand.

A smile touched the corners of Jayce's lips as he watched the cat.

It was then that he realised the conversation between Alexius and Iris had stopped and when he looked up, it was to see the both of them watching him and Fable. Oddly enough, Iris looked mystified. As if they were bearing witness to some inexplicable act of divinity and not simply Jayce petting a cat.

The expression on Alexius's face, meanwhile, was a bit trickier to discern. He seemed more focused on Jayce than Fable.

"Fable likes you," Iris said, more as a statement than a question, though they still sounded stupefied.

"Yes," said Jayce, watching his own fingers move against Fable's long, soft fur. "I suppose it does."

There was another pause, until, finally, Iris said, "All right. You can have the job."

"So, you're telling me that the reason Iris was so adamant about not having an assistant all this time . . . was because of the cat?"

It was nearing sundown, and he and Alexius were walking through the streets on their way back to the de Viccarri estate. After promptly announcing that they would be hiring Jayce as their assistant after all, Iris had spent the rest of the day showing Jayce the ropes of running the bookstore. They'd shown him how to take inventory, which books could be found where, what they needed to do to keep the book lice, away and made him watch as they dealt with the only two customers to wander into the store.

"Iris adores Fable," Alexius was saying now, as they walked past the street vendors packing up their stalls for the day and farmers heading down to one of the taverns after a hard day's work. "And she doesn't really take to strangers, so Iris didn't want to stress her out by having anyone else work in the shop. It took years before she warmed up to me."

"Hm."

"But she took to you straight away." Alexius was smiling at him. But there was something else in that smile that made Jayce feel flustered. Because it was like Alexius was looking at him as if he was a wonder.

"It must be my incredibly charming disposition," he said sardonically.

Alexius laughed, loud and uncaring of anyone who might look his way. Jayce's heart leapt at the sound of it.

"I agree," said Alexius. "You are very charming."

"You know, I can't be quite sure whether you're being serious or not."

In a much more earnest tone, Alexius replied, "Of course I am."

~

Working as Iris's assistant at *Tails and Tomes* was hardly a demanding job.

The store didn't get many customers, as Jayce soon came to realise over the next week. He thought that would probably explain why the shop looked full to bursting. But it also made him wonder how this place managed to stay afloat when it was doing so little business.

"I'm the only bookshop in Étoisaint," Iris said when Jayce asked them about it. "The Grand Duke thinks having at least one in this town makes it seem more cultured, so he pays a small sum to help keep me in business."

Jayce supposed that was fine by him. It meant that his days working at the bookshop were mostly dedicated to dusting shelves, reorganising books, keeping an eye out for book lice, and minding Fable when Iris wasn't around.

Jayce was standing behind the front counter, entertaining Fable with a piece of string he'd found, when he heard the front door's bell chime. He craned his neck to the side to see past one of the bookcases, in time to see the door swing shut and a small figure dart into the store.

Stepping out from behind the counter, and with his hands in his pockets, Jayce walked to the other end of the store, where he saw the newcomer disappear.

Crouched down behind one of the crooked stacks in front of the windows was a young girl with red hair tied into two plaits and wearing the blue and white uniform and buckled shoes of *D'Beau Artis*, Étoisaint's school.

She was also a dwarf, judging by her stocky stature and the

patches of red hair along the sides of her round face.

The girl looked startled to see him, staring up at him with blue eyes as wide as saucers, as if she hadn't expected to come barging into a shop and be confronted by one of the employees.

She was clutching something tight to her chest. A doll with button eyes and red yarn hair in a pink dress.

"This is a bookshop, you know?" Jayce said. "Not a place for you to play hide and seek."

"I'm not playing hide and seek," the dwarf girl snapped. "I'm just . . . hiding."

"From who?"

Before the girl could answer, she peered through the window, let out a squeaking sound and dashed behind one of the bookcases just in time for the bell to ring again and three more children to come rushing in. Two boys, one an elf, and a girl, all wearing the same blue and white school uniform. All with devilish little grins on their faces—at least until they spotted Jayce staring down at them.

"Here to buy some books, are you?"

"Um . . . not really," said the girl.

"Well, this is a bookstore and I see no reason why you might want to come in here if you weren't after some books."

"We were looking for a friend of ours," said the tallest boy with curly hair and a smattering of freckles.

"Yes," intoned the elf boy. "We thought we might have seen her come in here."

"She's a dwarf. With red hair. Have you seen her?"

"I'm just . . . hiding," the girl had said to him before. He might have thought she'd simply been lying to him about not playing any games, but then Jayce remembered the very real look of fear on her face when she'd caught sight of the other children. Something told him that these three weren't the friends they claimed to be.

"Can't say I have," said Jayce. "Now please, if you're not interested in buying anything, I'd prefer you didn't loiter around here."

With disappointed looks overlaying poorly concealed irritation, the children turned on their heels and exited the store. Jayce even looked out the window to make sure the three really had left, and was satisfied when he saw them disappear down the crowded street.

"Are they gone?"

He turned to see the dwarf girl's head sticking out from behind one of the bookcases.

"Yes," said Jayce.

The girl looked around nervously, as if she expected the other children to jump out at any moment. "Are you sure?"

"Quite sure. It's safe to come out now."

Hesitantly, the girl did so, clutching her yarn-haired doll in a nervous grip. "What makes you think I was worried it wasn't safe?" She asked, playing at bravado.

"Oh, I don't know, perhaps . . . *everything* about what just happened since you walked through this door."

The girl didn't have a retort. Instead, she looked sullenly at the floor with pinked cheeks.

"Those kids said you were a friend of theirs. Is that true?"

The girl shook her head.

"Didn't think so. Then why were they looking for you and why were you hiding from them?"

The girl remained tight-lipped.

Jayce sighed. "Come on, I let you hide out in my shop while I told a lie for you. I think you at least owe me some explanation."

"If I tell you, you'll just think I'm a scaredy-cat."

"No, I won't." And when the girl gave him a disbelieving look, he added, "I promise."

Still eyeing him distrustfully, the dwarf girl held out one of her hands and showed him her littlest finger. "Pinky promise?"

"Yes, uh . . . pinky promise." Jayce had no idea what such a thing was, but if it got this little girl to talk to him, then he'd promise on a finger if he had to.

Satisfied, she said, "Those three are always being mean to me.

They call me names and they pull my hair and trip me over." She lifted her skirt just enough to show Jayce the scabbed over wounds on her knees. "One of them pushed me over so that I ended up falling on some rocks. They also throw sticks at me sometimes, too."

"So they're bullying you. Have you told anyone about it?"

"My mothers found out about it. Then they got really upset and went to speak to the headmaster about it. But those three only behave badly when no one's around. So no one does anything about it."

The girl looked so small and hopeless; Jayce couldn't help but feel a stirring of pity for her. "Hm, in that case, I guess you can come to this shop whenever you need a place to hide."

Her eyes went as wide as saucers. "Really?"

"Only on the condition that you at least pretend to show some interest in the books here," Jayce said. "Otherwise, Iris, the one who owns this store, might get mad and throw you out."

"I promise," the girl beamed.

"Good. It might also do for me to know your name?"

"Maple. My name's Maple."

~

Maple ended up coming to the shop more frequently than Jayce expected. If it was not every day, then it was certainly every second day. Sometimes she even showed up in the middle of the day, which Jayce was certain was still during school hours.

True to her word, Maple did show an interest in the books on offer, and it seemed the interest was genuine. She took to one book in particular, a children's tale about a girl on board a pirate ship. Most of the time she could be found curled up in a corner of the shop, reading it.

When she wasn't doing that, Maple was busy shadowing Jayce, babbling to him about practically anything and everything. He learned that she was ten years old, and that her favourite colour was yellow. She used to have a pet cat, but it ran away. Her mothers owned a bakery on Her Lady's Lane. And that she'd had an older brother, but he had died two years back in the war and sometimes, she and her mothers still cried for him.

Her brother was also the one who gave her the doll she carried around everywhere.

"Do you have any brothers or sisters?" Maple asked Jayce while he was on the ladder, putting out book lice repellent on the top shelves.

"No," he said. "I was an only child."

"Just like me now. We're the same."

"I suppose we are."

Iris didn't mind having Maple hang around the shop. Jayce suspected they'd even developed a bit of a soft spot for her, which may have had something to do with the fact that Fable would sometimes sleep near her while she read her book about the girl pirate.

Alexius stopped by one afternoon while Maple was in the middle of telling Jayce and Iris about how her ma spilled a whole bag of flour the other night and started cursing like a sailor over the sandwiches Iris had made for them.

Jayce didn't think the girl's face could have gotten any redder when she first laid eyes on Alexius, dressed in his polished armour and red cape and his dimpled smile in place as he greeted them.

"So you're Maple?" he addressed the girl. "Jayce told me about you."

Maple could only make a sound like a mouse choking.

Alexius appraised her school uniform, and his smile turned slightly reprimanding. "School doesn't end for another three hours. You're not skipping, are you?"

"You're not going to scold her for it, are you, de Viccarri?" said Iris with an arch of their eyebrow. "Because I think that would be rather hypocritical of you, considering all the times you used to skip classes."

"The famous knight of Étoisaint has a rebellious past?" said Jayce. "How scandalous."

Alexius looked chastised. "Please don't talk about my dark past in front of the child."

Said child looked as if she were trying very hard not to giggle into her ham and lettuce sandwich.

Without warning, Alexius reached out across the counter and touched the knuckle of his finger to the corner of Jayce's mouth.

Jayce found himself frozen at the sudden contact, torn between batting Alexius's hand away and letting the touch linger.

"You had a crumb there," Alexius said.

Jayce feared he might go as red as Maple. "Thank you. I could have gotten it myself."

"Just trying to be helpful."

Alexius didn't stay for long, and after taking one of the remaining sandwiches for himself, he left.

"I didn't know you knew Alexius de Viccarri?" Maple was looking at Iris and Jayce with a newfound hero-worship.

"Oh yes," said Iris. "I've known the lug for quite some time now. And Jayce here is living with him."

"Are the two of you . . . *together*?" Maple asked Jayce.

"No," he said, perhaps a bit too quickly. "No, we're just . . . We're friends."

Jayce didn't miss the strange look Iris gave him.

~

The next time Maple came to *Tails and Tomes* her face was streaked with tears.

"Th-They—They took it," she sniffled while clinging to Jayce's leg.

He didn't have to guess who they were. "Took what?"

"My—My doll. The one my brother gave me. They took her off me while I was walking home and when I tried to get it back, they threw her down the hill and she disappeared into the woods. I-I wanted to go get her, but I was too scared. The teachers say never to go in there because a troll live in those woods."

Gently, Jayce drew Maple away by the shoulders, but only so he could look her in the face and ask, "Can you show me where?"

It was getting dark by the time Maple led Jayce back to the hilltop pathway she used to travel to and from *D'Baeu Artis*. And where she had lost her doll.

The path was canopied by overarching branches from the trees that lined one side. On the other side was a rather steep incline that led into a tangle of gnarled trees and bush.

"It was here," Maple pointed out to him.

"You're sure?"

The girl nodded. "I remember the flowers." She pointed to a patch of yellow wildflowers swaying lazily in the cool evening breeze by the side of the pathway.

"All right, you wait here. I'll see if I can find your doll," Jayce said before carefully making his way down the hill.

He passed the tree line and began searching through the prickly undergrowth. Thankfully, there was still just enough light out that he could see where he was looking. However, he could not see any sign of the doll with the red yarn for hair.

Just as Jayce was thinking a child couldn't have possibly thrown the toy that far, he spotted something in the earth that made his heart sink.

A set of footprints, twice as long and wide as any human's, were set deep into the earth right in front of him. They would have looked human-shaped, if not for the fact that the prints only had three toes instead of five.

A troll, Jayce realised miserably. Trolls weren't incredibly intelligent beings and were very reclusive. But they were also highly aggressive and territorial. Not to mention they were overly fond of collecting things, whether that be the sword from a fallen adventurer, or the skull of a decomposing animal, to a discarded glove. Or a child's toy.

Jayce couldn't think of a reason why a troll would be willing to wander so close to the edge of its territory unless it was for the doll.

"Did you find her yet?"

"I told you to wait," Jayce said, turning to face Maple.

"You were taking too long," she said.

He sighed. "I'm afraid your doll's lost for good. See those tracks? Those are from a troll. I think it's taken the doll."

Maple stared at the troll's footprints for a long time as Jayce's words sank in. Heartbreak gradually etched itself across her features.

"Then—Then we have to go after it," said Maple. "We can follow the footprints and get my doll back."

"You do understand how dangerous it is to confront a troll, don't you? And I don't even have a weapon on me."

"I don't care." Maple's eyes were brimming with tears. "I don't care. I won't let some stupid troll keep the doll my brother gave me. It's all I have left of him."

Jayce gazed down at the weeping Maple and felt his resolve to drag the girl kicking and screaming back to town crumble and fall away.

"All right," he said. "I'll find the troll and get the doll back. But I want you to go home."

"What? Why?"

"Because this could turn into a very dangerous venture and I'm not putting you at risk. Besides, it's getting late and I'm sure your mothers are starting to worry."

"But—"

Jayce held his hand up to stop anymore of Maple's protests. "Either you go, or I carry you back myself and I let that troll keep the toy."

Maple still looked conflicted about leaving Jayce, but ultimately his words seemed to have done the trick, and she turned on her heel and scrambled back up the hill.

Jayce waited a moment to be sure that Maple really had left. Once he was sure, he set off deeper into the woods.

The sun had completely set by the time Jayce had discovered the troll's lair deep in the forest. Fortunately, the moon was bright, making it easy for him to see where he was going.

And to see the shallow cave against a cliff face. Inside the cave, an already dying fire bathed the space in a flickering orange glow, allowing Jayce to see the impressive collection this troll had amassed for itself. There were clothes, torn and caked in dirt, strewn across the cave floor. Mismatched shoes, a horse's saddle, some hats, a longbow that had been snapped in two, flowers that were either wilting or already brown and wrinkled. He even spotted a few animal carcases that were in various stages of decay.

Amongst the odd and macabre collection was the troll. It was curled up on the ground by the cave wall with its green, wart-riddled back facing Jayce. He could hear its deep, rumbling snores even from where he stood behind a boulder outside of the cave, and determined that the beast must be asleep.

Unless he was willing to wait out here until morning, when— hopefully—the troll would get up and leave its den, now was likely the best time for Jayce to approach.

Keeping his tread as light and careful as possible, Jayce crossed the forest floor and into the troll's cave while it continued to slumber.

There was a putrid stench in the air, likely originating from the animal carcases, that almost made Jayce gag. Ignoring it as best he could, he cast about the troll's hoard for Maple's doll. He couldn't spot any sign of it and the last thing Jayce wanted to do was start digging through things. He was already on edge from the thought that his breathing alone would wake the troll.

But the more Jayce looked around, the more hopeless he grew that perhaps Maple's doll wasn't here.

The troll made a rumbling sound like falling rocks and Jayce's body—and his heart—went still as the troll shifted, turning over so its front was now facing Jayce. But the troll didn't open its eyes. It didn't wake at all. Its wide mouth, with two long, curling boar-like tusks, hung open as it snored loudly. Jayce relaxed.

At least until he saw what was clutched in the troll's obscenely large, leathery hands.

Maple's doll.

Well, isn't that perfect? he thought. Of course, the one thing Jayce had been willing to enter a troll's den for was currently being held by that very troll.

This was impossible, Jayce thought, preparing to back out of the cave. It was one thing to look for the doll when it might have simply been lying discarded in the troll's den, but to try and retrieve it from the troll's very clutches? He would be risking waking the beast and having it bite his head off more than he already was.

But then he remembered Maple, and the shattered look on her face when she had first come to Jayce to say that her doll had been stolen, and again when he'd told her they might never be able to get it back. He thought of her always carrying it around with her.

The last memento she had of her fallen brother.

Her brother, who had died in the war that Jayce had helped ensure lasted as long as it had.

If it wasn't for me, would Maple's brother still be alive?

The broken tip of a blade lay half buried in the dirt by his feet. He bent to pick it up. Though chipped and marked with age, it was still sharp.

Jayce wouldn't stand a chance of getting that doll out of the troll's firm grip, even while it slept. He had only one course of action and he could only hope it wouldn't end in a gruesome demise.

Adjusting his grip on the broken blade, Jayce plunged it into the troll's hand.

It awoke with an ear-shattering cry. It jerked upright and—just as Jayce had predicted—released its hold on the doll, dropping it to the ground.

Jayce didn't waste any time. He darted forward to scoop up Maple's doll.

And, when the troll inevitably turned its eyes—one bulbous, and one small—onto him, he did the only thing he could do.

He ran.

Despite its heavy, lumbering appearance, the troll was quick on its feet as it crashed through the forest after Jayce.

He heard the thunderous footfalls that shook the ground as if they were only a hairsbreadth behind him. Heard the violent shaking of leaves on their branches and the creaking and snapping of trees as the troll barrelled straight into them.

Even as Jayce tried to focus only on putting as much distance between himself and the troll as he was able to, he couldn't help but fear that it was impossible for him to outrun this thing.

And it was a stroke of supremely rotten luck that had Jayce's foot catch on a protruding tree root and send him sprawling onto the ground.

Jayce didn't have time to focus on the points of pain along his body. The troll would not allow him to. He only had enough time to turn onto his back before he saw the troll standing over him, holding its long arms above its head, prepared to bring them down to crush Jayce's skull in. The troll released a loud bellow and Jayce rolled to the side in time for the troll's fists to impact on the ground, where he had been only seconds before.

The troll didn't even give him the opportunity to find his feet again, and Jayce was forced to roll once, twice, three times more to avoid the enraged beast's fists from coming down on him.

Instead, they left some sizeable dents in the grass and dirt, making the ground beneath Jayce shudder so badly, he didn't even hear the pounding of approaching horse hooves, until he saw a familiar black gelding, and an even more familiar rider race up from behind the troll.

A pained roar left the troll as Alexius's sword caught it in the back as he rode past.

For a moment, Jayce was so shocked at the sight of Alexius that he just sat there staring with his mouth hanging open. Giving no thought to how he should use the opportunity to get up and away from the troll while it was distracted.

But even when it returned its attention to Jayce, Alexius didn't give it the chance to even try to attack again.

Having already wheeled Blackfire around, Alexius and his steed charged straight for the troll once more. Jayce dove out of Blackfire's path right before Alexius swerved his mount, avoiding the troll's outstretched arm.

In the split second where the beast lowered its arm, Alexius swung his sword out, the metal of the blade like a silver arc in the moonlight.

The next thing Jayce knew, the troll had gone still, its arms going limp at its sides as a thick line of red opened up along its squat neck.

A sheet of blood spilled down its front. The troll groaned, like the creaking of wooden rafters in a strong breeze, before it collapsed face first with an almighty thud.

The silence that followed felt just as loud as the commotion that had filled the air until now.

Blackfire trotted up to where Jayce was still sitting on the ground, clutching a child's toy. Alexius leapt from the saddle almost immediately, his armour clinking noisily.

"Are you all right?" he asked breathlessly, kneeling in front of Jayce.

Instead of answering, Jayce said, "What are you doing here?" He didn't mean to come off as ungrateful, but really, what were the chances that Alexius would just happen to be in these parts right when Jayce needed him?

"I ran into Maple while I was finishing up my shift," Alexius explained as he helped Jayce to his feet. "She told me about the toy and that you'd gone by *yourself* to retrieve it from a *troll*."

Jayce tried not to feel like a chastened child under Alexius's stern glare. "I had it under control."

"You did *not*."

"It doesn't matter now," he waved a hand flippantly. "What does matter is that I achieved what I set out to do, and I got Maple's doll back."

"Yes, you nearly got yourself killed just to get a toy back." Then he added in a softer tone, "I'm sorry. I was just . . . let's go, I'd rather not wait around for a second troll to show up."

Jayce almost pointed out that trolls were solitary, and it was likely Alexius had just killed the only one living anywhere near Étoisaint but decided to let it be. Tucking the doll into his belt, Jayce hoisted himself up onto Blackfire with Alexius riding pillion, his arms bracketing Jayce's waist so he could take hold of the horse's reins.

Even with the cold, hard press of Alexius's armoured front against his back, the position felt incredibly intimate. He could feel Alexius's warm breath against the shell of one ear. He repressed a shiver.

"Not so keen to give up the reins?" said Jayce as Blackfire began picking his way through the woods. "I am the one closest to them."

"I'd prefer you not to lead us into another life-threatening situation," Alexius deadpanned.

"But the night is still so young. I'm sure we have time to try and discover a drake's nest."

Another warm puff of air against his ear. A breath of laughter.

"You're impossible."

The words came out fond.

And it was that fondness that burrowed itself into Jayce's heart.

To say that Maple was happy to have her doll back was an understatement. When Jayce and Alexius arrived at the *Honey & Apple* bakery she and her mothers lived in sometime later, and the three dwarf women stepped out to see Jayce with the doll in his hands, Maple let out a shriek of delight.

"Thank you, thank you, *thank you!*" she cried loud enough to wake the entire street.

"Aye, thank you," said her mother, Honey, who had curly hair as red as her daughter and an accent that spoke of an origin beyond Solière. "We hope it wasn't too much trouble."

Jayce and Alexius exchanged a brief look and in that look they both decided not to mention the encounter with the troll.

"No," said Alexius with a dimpled smile. "It was no trouble at all."

"We thought the bullying had stopped," Apple said. She had a gruff voice, thick black hair, and the same blue eyes as Maple. "After we went to speak to the headmaster at the school, Maple stopped complaining about the bullying. And these last few days she seemed much happier. Even told us she'd made some new friends."

"But now we see we'll be needing to pay the headmaster another visit."

"Jayce."

He looked down. Maple was looking at him and when she made a gesture for him to come closer, he knelt down on one knee in front of her. No sooner had he done that, did Jayce find his arms full of the little dwarf girl who had thrown her arms around his neck.

"Thank you," she whispered, a wealth of meaning behind the words.

To have such gratitude directed towards him felt strange at first. But it quickly dissolved, giving way to the warm, pleasant feeling blooming in his chest. A gladness to see Maple so happy and the knowledge that he had been the one to put that smile on her face.

This one small act would not absolve him of all his past crimes, but for now, it was enough.

"You're welcome."

Chapter
Eleven

When Iris burst into the shop one afternoon, they appeared happier than Jayce had ever seen them. Jayce thought he could practically see excited sparks jumping off of them like embers leaping off a fire.

"Make sure you're up bright and early tomorrow morning, Jayce," Iris told him. "Because you and I are going on a trip."

"A trip to where?" Jayce asked as he went to rub Fable's belly, who was stretched out on the floor.

The cat immediately decided to attack the offending hand.

"To the Madame Alana Fréchnette's estate."

"Who?"

Iris held out a folded piece of crisp parchment and Jayce took it with the hand that wasn't currently being gnawed on.

In elegant, looping script, the letter read,

Dear Iris Ozveth,

    The Madame Alana Odette Géraldine Fréchnette, would like to invite you to her estate in Pré Fleurois. The Madame has expressed a wish to impart some her collection of books onto your store in

Étoisaint, free of any charge. Please feel free to stop by at your earliest convenience to peruse the Madame's collection.

On behalf of the Madame Alana Odette Géraldine Fréchnette,

The letter ended with a signature that looked more like a giant scribble to Jayce.

"She's the cousin of the Grand Duke," explained Iris. "Or maybe she's his aunt? I can't remember. Anyway, she has the most impressive collection of rare and valuable books this side of Solière!"

"You truly think this Madame Fréchnette is just going to give away her books?" he said sceptically.

"The Madame's on her deathbed." Iris took back the letter, slipping it back into the pocket of their coat. "And she has no children or relatives apart from the Grand Duke and his family, so it appears she has been simply giving away most of her riches. I heard just the other day that she allowed a gnome from some nearby village to take all six of her prized horses, along with enough money to care for them for life."

"And you really need me to come with you tomorrow?"

"You have not seen the Madame's book collection. I have, and there are so many, you'd probably have to spend years reading through them all. I can't possibly look over every single one on my own."

Jayce thought this might be the first time he had seen Iris smile so much since he'd first met them. "But what about the shop?"

"It won't hurt to close it for one day." Iris waved a hand dismissively. "It's not as if we get that many customers, anyway. Speaking of, have we had any today?"

"There were some young women in here before," Jayce said, disentangling his arm from Fable to reach for the cup of tea that sat on the counter behind him. "But they didn't buy anything."

The orc made a noise of disgust. "Most likely they were only in here to ogle my new assistant."

Jayce choked on his tea, and Fable looked up at him with startled eyes.

"No, it's settled," said Iris, unconcerned about Jayce's choking. "Tomorrow *Tails and Tomes* stays closed and you'll be joining me to Pré Fleurois."

~

At nearly the crack of dawn the next day, Jayce ventured to the town gates to meet Iris by the stables. The streets were quieter than Jayce had ever known them to be. Most shops hadn't even begun to open their doors yet, and he only came across two street vendors beginning to prepare their stalls for the day.

Iris was already waiting near the stables by the time he got there. Along with a piebald draught horse hitched to a cart. Surprisingly enough, he spotted Fable grooming herself on the horse's back.

Even more surprisingly, Alexius was standing by the cart as well.

"Iris asked me to accompany you both to Pré Fleurois," he told Jayce when asked of his presence here. "In case anyone should try to waylay you and all the precious cargo you'll be bringing home with you."

"So you're just hired muscle?"

"I suppose I am," said Alexius cheerfully.

"All right, we're all here, so let's get moving," Iris chimed in, already climbing onto the back of the cart with Fable draped across their shoulders like a furry, white scarf. "Get up the front, you big lug," they addressed Alexius. "You're driving."

It was quite the pleasant journey, Jayce had to admit. They rode out into the countryside where they were afforded a spectacular view of the sun breaking out over the fields and distant mountaintops. Chasing the night away, the first rays of sunlight began to paint the sky with pinks and light blues. The clouds streaked with purple, red and yellow. Jayce felt as if he were looking at the artwork of an exceptional painter, and it was almost hard to reconcile that this view did not come from the hand of a person but was rather a work of nature.

They passed farmers who were already getting to work in their fields. Many of whom raised a hand in greeting when they noticed their little party trundling past.

"Yesterday, you told me that you've already seen Madame Fréchnette's book collection," Jayce said to Iris, who was sitting across from him. "When was that?"

Iris adjusted their glasses. Fable was standing beside them on her hind legs, peering out over the cart. "Ah," they said. "It was quite a few years ago. When I was a child. The Madame invited the children of the orphanage to tour the Fréchnette estate. I think because our caretaker was her husband's niece or something or other. No doubt about it, my favourite part of the day was getting to walk through the library."

"Orphanage?" Of course, Jayce knew of the orphanage in Étoisaint, but it had never occurred to him that Iris—

"In case you haven't noticed, I don't have the typical stature that we orcs pride ourselves on so much." Iris reached over to pull Fable back when the curious feline began leaning too far over the edge of the cart, ignoring her meows of protest. "Even as a baby, I was apparently quite small for an orc. My parents must have been so horrified that they brought a runt like me into their family and dropped me on some poor old farmer's doorstep when I was only a few days old."

Jayce knew that orcs were . . . intense beings. And prized their physical strength above all else. Knowing that, he couldn't imagine one like Iris would have fit in well in orc society, but still, it seemed cruel that their parents would abandon them at so young an age because of their size.

"I'm sorry," Jayce offered.

"It could have been worse, I suppose. They could have just left me out in the woods to be eaten by panthers or wolves. And the orphanage was a nice enough place to grow up in. It's how I met my favourite lug, after all."

Jayce looked to Alexius, who was already giving him that dimpled smile from over his shoulder. "My grandmother was a patron of the orphanage, so I'd join her on her visits most of the time and made friends with the children there. It's how I met Joséphine, too."

"The first time we met, he bumped into me and made me drop the only book I owned into a great puddle of mud," said Iris.

"And then they started crying, so I took them into town and ended up buying three new books for them myself in apology," Alexius added.

"Those books were well worth the risk of getting caught sneaking out of the orphanage."

"Well, well," Jayce said to Alexius. "Seems you've always been quite keen to help others."

"I just didn't want my grandmother yelling my ear off for making one of the children cry."

"Oh, please," Iris said. "You have the biggest, softest heart in all of Solière."

Jayce found that he was inclined to agree wholeheartedly with Iris's statement.

Lush countryside soon gave way to vineyards and houses interspersed between the rows upon rows of grapevines. Jayce spotted workers here and there, picking from the vines and carrying wooden buckets full of plump purple grapes. On the road, they passed a weather-beaten old man wearing a sun hat, leading a donkey carrying two small barrels on either side of its grey body. Fable hissed in Jayce's lap at the sight of the donkey.

Seeing these people working in the vineyards stirred a memory in Jayce. Of the apple orchard he'd lived on as a boy. Of workers like these, pulling bright red apples from their branches and placing them in large baskets, their figures sun-dappled by the trees.

He could hear these orchard workers' voices speaking indistinct words, and laughing with each other as they worked. It gave Jayce a feeling of happiness, which was quickly quelled by his bitterness at barely being able to remember these moments of his past.

Jayce kept his head down and his eyes on the cat in his lap for the rest of the trip.

It was late morning by the time they reached the Fréchnette estate. A tall white building with blue rooftops and gilded window frames, sitting proudly on top of a green hilltop that protruded from the maze of vineyards.

"Do you want me to wait by the cart?" Alexius asked as they pulled up to the front of the mansion.

"I brought you along to put those tree trunk arms of yours to use and that is what I intend to do," Iris said, demonstratively putting their hand on one of Alexius's impressive biceps.

Fable leapt out of the cart after Jayce and immediately darted into one of the nearby hedgerows.

"She'll be fine," said Iris. "She doesn't get the chance to explore new places that often, after all."

It wasn't long after that a footman, dressed in a spotless black coat with gold buttons and a white powdered wig upon his head, was stepping out of the mansion's front doors to greet them.

"You are Iris Ozveth, yes?" asked the footman. "From the bookshop in Étoisaint?"

"Yes. And this here is my assistant and our guard."

"Very good. Please, if you will all come with me, I shall show you to the library."

The footman brought them through the vast halls of the mansion, full of crystal chandeliers, opulent furniture and balustrades, and skirting boards with intricate details carved into them. The heels of the footman's shoes echoed against the polished floors with every step he took.

"I hope you understand that the Madame will not be joining us during your visit today," explained the footman. "As she is in far too weak a state to leave her bed."

"Of course," said Alexius, while at the same time offering a smile to a passing maid with an armful of laundry. The young woman promptly flushed red and buried her shy smile into the clothing she was carrying. Jayce rolled his eyes.

Finally, they reached the end of a wide corridor, where a pair of large doors awaited them. The footman pushed them open, and Jayce was helpless to stop his jaw from falling open at the sight that awaited them.

After spending many years of his life living in a castle, he was no stranger to grandiose architecture. What really caught him by surprise was the sight of such a vast collection of books.

The room was all white. White floors and white walls. White bookcases embedded in the walls, climbing all the way up to the domed ceiling that towered a great deal above their heads. There were no windows, but there was a skylight in the high ceiling. A circle of sunlight glowed on the floor directly below it.

Foolishly tall ladders clung to the bookcases, so as to allow one to reach the books even on the very top shelves, which looked at least three storeys high. Jayce couldn't imagine anyone with a fear of heights would dare to brave those ladders.

When Jayce tore his gaze away from the sheer number of books before them, he looked at Iris and Alexius. Iris had stars in their dark brown eyes and an incandescent brightness about their expression that was wholly unfamiliar to Jayce. They gazed at these books the way a drake might at their hoard of treasure, or a sailor, too long on land, at the open sea.

Alexius looked marginally less enthused. Although, that was not to say that he didn't appear impressed at all by this marvel of a library. In fact, he showed a rather respectable amount of polite admiration on his face for one who did not care much for books.

"Please, feel free to take as many or as few books as you desire," said the footman. "I'll leave you with two attendants, Philipe and Vivienne." He gestured to the two servants—one a round-faced human, and the other a dark-skinned elf woman—who had appeared in the doorway behind them. "They shall assist you in whatever you need during your time here."

With that, the footman took his leave.

Iris got straight to work, commandeering the two attendants for their own, and leaving Jayce and Alexius to peruse the extensive collection by themselves.

Before they had even arrived at the estate, Iris had already given Jayce leave to take whatever books he wanted, whether for his own personal collection or to take back to the shop. Jayce was all too happy to spend most of his time searching for books to keep for himself.

After the first hour, he already had a pile of seven books he would be stowing away in his bedroom at the de Viccarri estate.

He was walking back to the little nook he had sequestered himself in with a new book in hand, and came to a halt when he saw Alexius there.

The knight was sitting on the floor beside the armchair Jayce had occupied, with his legs crossed and his head bent over an open book in his lap. His brow was creased in a look of concentration, and Jayce couldn't keep himself from smiling at the sight. It was just so endearing.

Alexius didn't look up from the pages until Jayce was standing right in front of him, and when he finally did acknowledge Jayce's presence, he looked startled.

"Ah, Jayce. I didn't see you there."

"Were you truly that engrossed?" Jayce asked with a raised eyebrow.

"Yes—I mean no. Not engrossed exactly . . ."

Alexius was in the middle of closing the book he was reading, already moving to set it aside. Before he could, Jayce reached out and deftly plucked it from Alexius's hands, being sure not to lose the page Alexius was on.

"Wait, don't—" Alexius made a half-hearted attempt to reach for the book, but Jayce had already seen it.

On the first page was a long column of fine, black script, the edges embossed in gold. There were no words on the next page. But there was an illustration. Drawn exquisitely in black ink was a depiction of a naked man leaning against a garden wall, his head was tipped up with his eyes closed and his mouth open. Jayce was sure it had to do with the other man kneeling before him, also without a single article of clothing and with his dark-haired head pressed between the first man's legs.

Turning the book over to take a look at its cover, Jayce read the title printed in scarlet lettering, *The Seduction of Olivier Lopault*.

"Well," said Jayce mildly. "I'm not sure whether I really should be shocked that erotic tales are your book of choice."

"It's not like that," Alexius defended. "I was simply admiring the illustrations."

"I bet you were."

"Oh, stop." Alexius snatched the book out of his hands and set it aside. "What book do you have there?"

He was only trying to change the topic of conversation from the erotic novel, Jayce knew. But he decided to indulge him, nonetheless.

He handed the book to Alexius, who read the title aloud, *"Tales from Over the Rosebush by Auguste du Lacsbourg."*

"It's a children's story," said Jayce as he sat down on the floor in front of Alexius. "One of my favourites when I was younger."

"I thought you didn't remember the books from your childhood?"

"I don't." Jayce had to ignore the brief prick of annoyance he felt at the reminder. "But there were times when I was given days off from all the training the Dark Lord put me through. Before I became Grey. Days where I could do whatever I wanted, and usually what I wanted to do on those days was lose myself in a good book." He took the book back from Alexius. "This was one of them."

Alexius had a somewhat dubious frown on his face. "The Dark Lord gave you books?"

"Hard to believe someone like him gifting a child with books, isn't it? For those first few years, I believe he wanted me to think of him as some kind of father figure. Of course, I refused to and, in the end, he gave up. It was enough for him to have my loyalty through the collar."

Unconsciously, he lifted his hand to trace one the scar that ringed the base of his throat, but quickly dropped it into his lap again when he realised what he was doing.

Jayce didn't dare look up at Alexius to see if he had noticed.

"This book is about two brothers," he went on to explain. "Louis and Lionel, whose mother is kidnapped by a witch and the brothers have to travel into a hidden world that exists beyond the large rosebush in their garden, to save her. They have all sorts of adventures and while some of them are scary and dangerous, Louis and Lionel always have each other."

Jayce traced his fingers along the golden silhouettes of two boys walking hand in hand on the cover. "Even when they fight, they're always there to keep each other safe. I used to think that if they could endure things like almost getting eaten by giants or battling evil witches, then I could endure too—sorry. I was rambling too much, wasn't I?"

"No, not at all," Alexius said with a shake of his head. "I—I enjoy it. Getting to hear your thoughts and about your past."

"Why would you enjoy hearing of my past? Everything that I can remember properly is rather depressing."

"I know that, and I'm sorry you went through all that. But it helps me understand you a little better." Looking suddenly bashful, Alexius rubbed at the back of his neck, his gaze cast to the side. "I like the idea of being closer to you. As much as you'll let me."

Jayce felt as if Alexius had reached into his chest and stolen the breath from his lungs. Why did he have to say such things? Things that only made the flame of Jayce's affections for Alexius burn all the more brighter. This was all uncharted territory for Jayce, and he wasn't sure how he would be able to handle it if the flame grew even stronger.

"You'll be taking that book home with you, I assume?" Alexius asked, nodding at *Tales from Over the Rosebush* in Jayce's lap.

"Your assumption is correct."

"Good. Do you mind if I read it?"

"For after you've finished reading your erotic novels?"

"Shut up."

They did not leave Madame Fréchnette's estate until the sky had started to grow dark. Fable was already waiting for them by the time they started loading the books into the cart, sitting upon the driver's seat while she licked her fluffy tail.

The amount of books they were bringing back to Étoisaint with them meant that on the ride back, Jayce and Iris had to sit squeezed in between the stacks.

With the edge of a book digging almost painfully into his arm, Jayce thought it was fortunate they had brought the large draught horse with them. A smaller breed might not have been able to pull such a heavily laden cart like this on its own without tiring quickly.

Movement drew his eye to where Fable had leapt up onto one of the stacks boxing him in. She sat down, curling her tail around her paws, and gazed down at him with a lazy expression. Jayce imagined that she was gloating about her freedom to move about unrestricted, while he was squashed into an uncomfortable position.

I envy you, he mused with a half-smile at the cat. Then he craned his neck to peer around the pile of books so he could see where Alexius sat on the driver's seat. Also free from being squished by books. *And I envy you, too.*

Jayce tried to tell himself that was why his eyes lingered longer than they needed to on Alexius's broad back and the way the waning sunlight outlined his figure in gold.

By the time they returned to Étoisaint and helped Iris transfer all of the books from the cart and into the bookstore, it was getting late into the night, and Jayce felt as wrung out as a used dish towel. Taking a warm bath almost as soon as he returned to Alexius's estate only served to make him even more drowsy.

Dressed in his bedclothes, which consisted of an overlarge white shirt and soft pants, Jayce padded down the dark hallway towards his bedroom, ready to collapse onto the soft mattress and have it carry him into a blissful slumber.

Until he saw candlelight still burning from the open doorway of Alexius's bedroom.

When he took a look inside, it was to see Alexius sitting on the divan by the window, reading *Tales from Over the Rosebush*.

"Neglecting your erotic novel already?"

Alexius looked up and his expression went from surprised to sour in a handful of seconds. "I didn't even take that bloody book, and you know it," he grumbled.

Jayce hummed. "A shame." He pushed away from the doorway and crossed the carpeted floor to perch himself on the edge of Alexius's ridiculously large bed. A bit daring of him, perhaps, but Alexius didn't seem to mind.

"A blessing," the other man said. "I can only imagine how much worse your taunts would have been if I really had decided to keep that book."

A smile tilted Jayce's lips, because Alexius wasn't wrong. "How are you finding this one, then?"

"I've only just started." Alexius looked back down at the open pages before him. "It seems like a story more suited to children."

Jayce tried and failed to stifle a yawn. "You don't have to read it if it's not to your taste, you know?" When had he laid down? The bedcovers were so soft and warm beneath his cheek.

"I never said that it *wasn't* to my taste. But even so, I want to keep reading it. Because you said that it was one of your favourites—"

Had Alexius's voice always been so soothing? Jayce soon found that he could no longer keep his eyes open, his lids having grown too heavy.

He was asleep before he knew it.

When Jayce next woke up, sometime in the early hours of the

morning, he found himself in his own bed, tucked beneath the blankets.

For the next few days, whenever Alexius was not otherwise preoccupied, he could usually be found with his nose stuck in *Tales from Over the Rosebush*.

One morning, Alexius even brought it to the table to read over breakfast.

"I need to know how Louis makes it out of the labyrinth before the beast reaches Lionel," Alexius said fervently when Abby warned him that his porridge was going cold.

It was a bit baffling to see, but it also made Jayce's heart glad to see Alexius grow so attached to a story that had been dear to Jayce for some time. He also thought it made him fall a little bit deeper in love with Alexius—if such a thing was even possible.

Jayce was in the middle of closing up the bookshop for the day when Alexius came barging in, dressed in plain clothes and with an extremely troubled look on his face. Jayce felt real concern for a moment, until Alexius opened his mouth to say, "How could the book end like that?"

For a moment, all Jayce could do was blink. "What?"

"Louis and Lionel's mother *died*."

"Oh. Yes, she does die, doesn't she?"

"And after everything they went through to try and save her, and she dies!" Alexius shot him an accusatory glare. "I thought you said it was a children's story?"

"It *is* a children's story. But the world isn't always so kind to children either."

"I know that, but this is fiction," said Alexius. "Isn't the point of reading something fictional to make you feel as if you're in a world that's better than our own?"

"Not always," Jayce said. "I've read plenty of fictional tales that were quite tragic but still rather enjoyable."

Alexius just looked at him as if he had all of a sudden sprouted a pair of feathery wings or a second head.

As they walked home through the streets, Alexius continued to bemoan the ending of the book.

"I did enjoy it, however," he was saying. "I only wish it could have had a happier ending. Next time you give me a book to read, please make sure it has a happy ending."

"Noted."

They'd come to the town square, which was beginning to empty of people as the working day came to a close. As he and Alexius passed through the square, Jayce noticed that a man with a few rolls of parchment beneath one arm was in the middle of pinning one to the notice board, by the wall of the tavern.

Curiosity piqued, Jayce went over to have a look at it with Alexius trailing behind him.

The first thing Jayce noticed about the new sheet of crisp, white parchment pinned amongst all the other squares of yellowed, and weather-worn papers, was the sketched portrait on the bottom.

Detlas, he realised with a shock.

Because he would recognise that brutish, flat-nosed face anywhere.

Above the portrait, read the words,

Dear citizens of Étoisaint,

    Detlas de Monte, the former general of the Dark Lord's army, has been spotted in the surrounding regions. We warn the townsfolk to stay vigilant as authorities work to apprehend this man. De Monte is an extremely dangerous individual, therefore, we must warn that, should anyone encounter him, not to try and engage with him. Instead, report straight to the town guard.

The message was signed off with the Grand Duke's swan seal.

"He's here," the words slipped out of Jayce's mouth of their own accord. He couldn't take his eyes off of the notice. Off Detlas's face drawn on paper. *Gods. I was certain he would have died after that wound I dealt him. How did he survive?*

"What is he doing all the way out here?" said Alexius.

But Jayce already knew the answer. He remembered his last encounter with Detlas during the battle at the Dark Citadel. *"Mark my words, Grey. You won't get away with this. I will make you pay for betraying us this day."*

It seemed that Detlas really meant to make good on his promise.

A gentle hand on his shoulder and Jayce realised that Alexius had been calling his name. "What?"

"You've gone almost white." There was concern in Alexius's features as he looked down at Jayce.

"Have I?"

Alexius's hand on his shoulder became firmer, more grounding and reassuring. "They'll find him. *I'll* find him. I won't—I told you; you would be safe here. And I'm going to make sure of it."

Even if only for a moment, Jayce allowed himself to trust in Alexius's words.

Chapter
Twelve

Spring was in full swing. The sky was as blue as a polished gemstone and the breeze had a pleasant warmth to it.

The whole of Étoisaint seemed to be infected with the brightness of the day. The streets were brimming with more people than usual for this time of day. The laughter of children playing carried through the air. Along with birdsong and the hawking of vendors. Somewhere in the distance, a bard struck up a melody in the street,

Jayce was making his way down the bustling laneway of Bower Street, heading back to *Tails and Tomes* after a quick lunch break of warm bread, soft cheeses, and salted cuts of meat at *Honey and Apple*.

"We do have other food here you can order, you know?" Maple's mother, Apple, had said to him, after Jayce had ordered exactly the same dish as he always did each time he went there. But she said it to him in a teasing way rather than as an admonishment, and it struck Jayce in that moment that he had stopped by regularly enough for her to joke with him like that. That he was familiarising himself with the people of Étoisaint. That Étoisaint was starting to become like a home to him.

The amicable chatter that surrounded him as he walked was

pierced by a commotion in one of the side streets to Jayce's left.

"Thief!" The cry went up. "Stop! Thief!"

A young man in a dark cloak came barrelling out onto the main street, roughly shoving past people as he did so.

The thief came close enough to Jayce that he was able to stick his foot out and send the man flying to the ground. A satchel fell as well, spilling coin purses and pieces of jewellery to the cobblestones.

The thief scrambled to his feet. "Who did that?" he looked around wildly before his eyes landed on Jayce. "You. You're gonna regret that."

He pulled out a battered-looking knife from his belt and lunged at Jayce.

Jayce may not have been in possession of immense magical powers anymore, but his lessons in hand-to-hand combat and swordplay had been too brutally ingrained into him for the instincts to go away any time soon.

As soon as he saw the blade come out, it was as if his body had been taken over by a puppeteer, and he needed very little thought to go behind his movements.

Once the thief was close enough, knife arm outstretched, ready to drive the blade through his gut, Jayce grabbed the man by the wrist. While he allowed the thief's momentum to carry him forward, Jayce moved behind him, bringing the thief's knife arm with him.

As the thief stumbled backwards, Jayce twisted his wrist just enough to elicit a pained curse and for the knife to clatter to the ground.

"I'm sorry," said Jayce. "What was I supposed to regret again?"

That was when the guards finally decided to show up, calling out to the gathered crowd to make way as they moved in to clap the thief in irons.

Jayce stepped back, releasing his hold on the thief only when the two guards had him. He and the rest of the onlookers watched as the thief was led away, struggling and spitting venom.

"All right, everyone," said one of the guards, retrieving the thief's stolen goods and the knife. "The spectacle is over. Go back to your business."

And—almost hesitantly—that is just what everyone did.

Jayce was about to as well when an unfamiliar voice called out to him.

"That was bold of you," said a young man in richly tailored clothing. Detaching himself from the rest of the crowd to amble towards Jayce. "Taking on someone armed like that."

"He was the one who came at me," Jayce explained. "I merely defended myself."

The man smiled at him. He was perhaps only a little older than Jayce. He was also an elf. The point of one ear peeking out between the fall of his jaw-length, brown curls.

"And I must confess, I do not know of many civilians who would know how to defend against such attacks."

"My father was a knight," Jayce lied smoothly. "From Thelos. He thought it wise to impart his skills before he passed."

A sympathetic look crossed the elf's features. "My condolences."

"It happened a long time ago."

The elf nodded to himself. He stepped closer towards Jayce. He was taller by only a few inches. "You know," he said with a slow, curling smile. "I would not mind seeing exactly what your father taught you."

Wait. Was this strange elf . . . flirting with him?

"Jayce!"

Behind him, he spotted none other than Alexius, dressed in his rose-gold armour, and rushing through the crowd towards him.

"I heard about an incident with a thief pulling out a knife on someone," he said once he was close enough. "Are you all right?"

Alexius looked so genuinely concerned about him and Jayce wasn't sure whether he was touched by it, or a bit put out that Alexius would think he couldn't handle a mere thief.

"How did you know I was the recipient of this attack?" He asked with a tilt of head.

Alexius's expression softened into a fond smile. "I heard people talking about how this heroic person disarmed the scoundrel without even batting an eye and I just knew it had to be you." He lifted his hand, as if he meant to touch Jayce, before he quickly dropped it again, looking startled with himself.

Jayce couldn't help but take particular notice of the aborted action.

"Alexius." The elf's voice reminded Jayce of his presence. "It's been a long time, friend."

"Florent." Alexius beamed, opening his arms and the two men exchanged a brief embrace. "Gods, I didn't notice you there for a moment."

With a laugh and wry smile, Florent said, "I could see that." His gaze flitted briefly to Jayce. "So, I see you know this newest hero?"

Jayce scowled at being called a hero, while Alexius said, "Indeed. This is Jayce. I met him in the Dark Citadel. He's been staying with me at the estate for the time being."

"Ah, yes. I'd heard tell of as much."

"Jayce," Alexius said, "This is Florent. An old friend of mine from the Crown City. He's one of the Queen's knights."

Jayce nodded his head at the elf. "A pleasure."

"The pleasure is all mine."

"And what brings you all the way from the Crown City?" asked Alexius.

"I'm on leave and I thought, why not use the time to do some travelling? Maybe pay a visit to my old friend, Alexius, in Étoisaint? Perhaps we can catch up some time over a drink? I can tell you about my adventures in the Crown City and you can regale me with the epic battle at the Citadel?"

"Well, I was locked in a dungeon for most of it, so I'm not sure how epic my version of events would be, but consider your offer accepted."

"Excellent," said Florent. "And I so hope you'll join us as well, Jayce?"

There was that look again. "Oh, I don't know," Jayce said airily. "Iris has quite a hold on my time at the moment."

"Iris? That orc with the cat who detests me?"

"The very same," said Alexius.

"Well, never fear," Florent announced. "Should the need arise, just leave them to me. I'll get them to let you out of their grasp for a moment or two."

With a smile and wink that Jayce imagined would have left quite the number of people weak in the knees, Florent departed.

~

After that day in Bower Street, Jayce began to see more of Florent. True to his word, he invited Jayce and Alexius out for dinner and drinks in the more luxurious tavern in Étoisaint.

There, Jayce learned that Florent's full name was Florent Feydellen. The second eldest son of a renowned playwright, Lawrence Feydellen.

He told them tales of the opulence of the Crown City and the Queen's court. The people he met and even the people he bedded. In exchange, Alexius told him of the battles he fought against the Dark Lord's forces, his capture, and the battle at the Citadel, only mentioning Jayce as someone he had met while trapped for weeks in the dungeons.

When asked about his own story, Jayce stuck to the part lie he and Alexius had agreed upon. That he had been taken prisoner by the Dark Lord and was suffering from partial memory loss.

"Perhaps I was caught trying to storm the Citadel single-handedly," Jayce joked.

"I do hope not," said Florent. "For that sounds unspeakably foolish, and I would like to think you have better sense than that."

At that point, Jayce had been beginning to feel the effects of the alcohol he had been drinking and was feeling prone to dramatics.

"What is life if one doesn't court a bit of danger from time to time? Dull, I tell you!"

Florent had thrown his head back and laughed. "True indeed, my dear Jayce."

For the rest of their night together, Florent had cast Jayce admiring looks—which Jayce pretended not to notice.

Meanwhile, Alexius had grown quieter and quieter. Something dark in his expression as he watched Jayce and Florent.

Again, Jayce pretended not to notice.

The next he saw of Florent was not even two days later, when he walked into the shop on a late afternoon while Jayce was left alone with Fable to mind things. He mostly subjected Jayce to small talk, at which point Jayce wished desperately for even just one customer to walk through the door so he would have an excuse to extract himself from the conversation.

After that, Florent started visiting the bookshop daily. Sometimes as if he simply wished to enjoy the company of Jayce and even Iris— apparently the two already had met a few years ago, the first time Florent visited Étoisaint. Other times he did query Jayce about the books that were on offer in the store, though he never actually bought anything.

"What sort of books do you like?" Florent asked him once while Jayce was in the middle of reorganising one of the top shelves.

"I like just about any book, really," he answered.

"But surely you have to have a favourite? Romance perhaps?"

"No." It wasn't that Jayce had anything against those sorts of books, really. The few he had read had simply not been to his tastes. "I like poetry."

"Isn't most poetry about romance?"

"Poetry can be about many things. Such as war, grief. Even cats." He spared a scritch under the chin for Fable, who was stalking the shelves, eying Florent balefully.

"Hm," was all Florent had to say on the matter.

~

Nearly a week later, on one stunning morning while Jayce and Alexius ate their breakfast together, Estelle entered, carrying a rectangular parcel, she said had just been brought round by the courier.

"It's for you, Jayce," she told him, handing him the parcel.

Jayce cleared a space on the table and set the package down. Whatever it was, it was exquisitely wrapped in paper as red as a ruby and shimmering like an oil slick. It was adorned with a white ribbon tied into a bow.

"What is it?" Alexius asked, leaning over to inspect.

"Let's find out." Tugging on the bow, Jayce undid the ribbon.

As the wrapping paper fell away, it revealed a white box beneath and inside, when Jayce lifted the lid, was a book, nestled in silk-fine wads of pink paper that gave off the faintest scent of rosemary.

The book was a gorgeous thing, Jayce noticed right away. Simply by looking at its emerald-green cover, embossed with gold patterns, he could tell that it would easily fetch a price of at least eight hundred gold coins.

In gold curling lettering, the title on the front read, *Blooming in Midnight – A Poetry Collection*.

Jayce sucked in a breath. This wasn't from who he thought it was, was it?

He lifted the book out of its box and began perusing through the pages, with Alexius looking over his shoulder. Even the inside of the book was immaculate, its pages free of any sort of creases and they were perfectly white with gold edges.

"Who sent you this?" Alexius said after some time of page flipping.

As if to answer his question, something fell out from between the pages and into Jayce's lap. A slip of paper.

Lifting it up to inspect, Jayce discovered there were words written on it in slanted handwriting.

I know you said you did not like romance,
but this one in particular reminded me of you.
— F.

F. So this *was* sent to him by Florent.

He returned his attention to the book, still open on the same page Florent's note had fallen from.

Appearing in my dreams

Your face I would know anywhere

Love. So it is real.

"Gods," said Alexius once Jayce had finished reading. "He's truly courting you, isn't he?"

Before Jayce could turn around and say a word, he saw that Alexius was already walking out of the dining room.

∼

It was a miserable day. Grey and pouring rain, with rumblings of thunder in the distance. The beginnings of a spring storm.

Jayce sat in one of the wingback armchairs by the window in the drawing room, watching the rivulets of rain snake their way down the windowpanes and thinking how it was lucky Iris had given him the day off today.

Estelle had been by only moments before to offer to light the fire in the hearth if he was too chilly, but Jayce had refused. He did not think the air was cool enough to warrant a fire, let alone the effort of lighting one.

Open in his lap was *Blooming in Midnight,* the book that Florent had sent to him days ago.

The book that was clearly meant to be a courting gift.

He was still unsure what he was supposed to do with it—did he send it back to Florent? Or could he keep it even though he had no plans of accepting Florent's courtship? He hoped it was the latter. It was a fine book, and he was enjoying the variety of poems contained within.

What would Alexius think if I kept it?

Jayce often found his thoughts wandering back to the morning the book had come. When Florent's note had fluttered out from between the pages, finally making his intentions towards Jayce clear.

"Gods. He's truly courting you, isn't he?"

Alexius's reaction had baffled him then. He'd been . . . not upset, exactly. But something about Florent's gift had clearly bothered him. And it bothered Jayce a great deal that he could not put his finger on it.

Was Alexius jealous, perhaps? But why would he be? As far as Jayce was aware, his feelings for Alexius were entirely one-sided.

Or were they? He still remembered the way Alexius had reached for him that day after his encounter with the thief.

Jayce was brought out of his musings by the sound of music drifting through the house. *A piano,* he realised.

The notes were soft and lulling. With an almost haunting air to their melody.

Closing the book, Jayce set it down as he rose from the armchair. Padding out of the drawing room and out into the hallway, following the sounds of the piano.

It led him upstairs. He made his way through the winding corridors, darkened by the weak light outside, until he came to the one room he hadn't set foot in since he'd first arrived here. The piano room. It was sparsely furnished with a large embroidered rug taking up most of the floor. The walls were painted a burgundy colour with three tall windows.

In the centre of the room was a grand piano and, sitting on the bench, in front of the keys, was Alexius.

Jayce stood in the doorway, simply watching Alexius. He was dressed plainly, in a pair of dark trousers and a white cotton shirt, sleeves rolled up to the elbow. His fingers glided effortless and elegant over the piano's ivory keys. His head was bent forward, his expression relaxed. It took Jayce a moment before he realised that Alexius had his eyes closed. Like he was lending himself over completely to the music.

Jayce stayed where he was until Alexius's playing came to an end.

"That's the first time I've heard you play," he said.

Alexius jerked in his seat and when he turned to look at Jayce, the look on his face was so startled that Jayce burst out laughing.

"What's so funny?" asked Alexius.

"Nothing. Nothing." Jayce moved away from the doorway and came to sit on the bench beside Alexius.

"It's been a long time since I last played," Alexius said, addressing Jayce's earlier statement. His fingers drifted lightly over the keys, as if taking in the feel of them. "Probably not since before the war started."

Inexplicably, Jayce felt a burgeoning guilt at the idea that a war started by his former master, the war where he had fought on the wrong side, had been what kept Alexius from something he loved for so long.

"The war's been over for some time now," he said carefully. "And you've been home for a while now, too."

"I know. I don't know why it's taken me so long to play again. I think maybe I was afraid that I wouldn't remember after all this time."

"Remember how to play?"

"That I wouldn't remember how it feels." Before Jayce could ask what he meant by that, Alexius carried on. "I told you that my grandmother was the one to teach me how to play the piano and that playing it was one of our favourite things to do together. I was always happiest when I sat here, creating music with her. And I—I'm not quite sure how to describe it exactly. But that feeling was so precious to me. I was afraid that if I sat here and tried to play after the war, after she was gone, it just wouldn't be the same, and I'd forget just how happy I was when I was playing with her." He let out a weak laugh. "Sorry. I probably sound silly, don't I?"

"No," Jayce said without hesitation. "You don't sound silly at all. After everything that's happened, after everything you lost, it makes sense that you would want to hold on to the happiness you had before."

Alexius seemed taken aback by Jayce's response. He did nothing but look at Jayce in stunned curiosity before returning his gaze back to the piano keys.

"Even so, there are plenty of other things that make me happy now."

"Like what?" Jayce asked unthinkingly, watching Alexius's hands move softly over the keys.

"Like you."

Jayce's head shot up at the same time Alexius's did. He imagined that his own expression could be mirrored by Alexius's, who was looking at him with wide eyes and parted lips. As if he too was caught off guard by his words.

"What?" Jayce asked, his voice whisper soft.

Alexius's chest was rising and falling at a quicker pace than usual beneath his white shirt. "I—You make me happy, Jayce. When I'm with you, I always feel in high spirits. You make me laugh. And I think if you weren't here, I'd be very lonely. Your company is something I truly cherish."

It was no declaration of love. Far from it. Yet it set Jayce's heart to racing and flushed a pleasant warmth beneath his skin. To hear the man he loved say that he treasured Jayce, that Jayce made him happy. Even if it was not the same as hearing Alexius say that he was in love with Jayce as well, it was still enough. It was enough for him to know that he did have a place in Alexius's heart, even if it was only a small one.

It was enough.

"Will you play something for me?" he asked Alexius after a while.

A slow smile spread over Alexius's face. "For you, anything."

For the rest of the day, the old house was filled with piano music and occasionally punctuated with laughter.

Jayce knew that rainy afternoon would be imprinted in his memory as one of the happiest moments in his life.

Chapter
Thirteen

It was an ordinarily slow day at *Tails and Tomes*. Jayce had just sent off their first and only customer of the day—an old dwarf looking for the perfect book to give to his great-grandson—when Alexius waltzed in. Straight up to the counter where Jayce was still depositing the four silver coins from the old dwarf's purchase into the strongbox.

"The Grand Duke is celebrating his fiftieth in three days' time," Alexius announced. "And I've been invited to the celebrations at his home."

"Good for you," said Jayce.

"And I was hoping you would like to attend with me?"

Of course, Jayce was surprised by the invitation. He would have thought Alexius might prefer to bring someone more befitting of that sort of company. Such as one of the pretty young ladies who enjoyed fawning over the handsome young knight of Étoisaint.

"Are you sure it's wise for me to attend the Grand Duke's party?" Jayce asked instead.

"Why wouldn't it be?"

He gave Alexius an arched look.

"Oh!" Alexius said with sudden realisation. "Of course it'll be fine. Jayce, you've been here nearly a whole season and not a soul has ever recognised you as anyone other than the young man who works in the bookshop. If they even recognise you at all."

"Why thank you," Jayce deadpanned.

"I'm just telling you; you don't have to worry about that. So, what do you say? Will you come with me to the party?"

Jayce thought it over some more before he finally said, "I suppose."

~

They took a carriage to the Grand Duke's house on the night of his fiftieth birthday celebrations.

"Are you sure I don't look ridiculous in this?" Jayce asked, trying, and failing, to catch a glimpse of his reflection in the glass of the carriage windows. It was too dark out.

"Of course not. I picked the clothes out myself, didn't I?" said Alexius.

"That's why I'm concerned."

Alexius made an affronted noise. "Now that's just hurtful."

Jayce hid a smile behind his hand. There was truly nothing wrong with the clothes. He simply enjoyed giving Alexius a hard time.

The clothing he wore now was some of the finest he had ever worn. He was dressed entirely in rich, dark blue. A doublet with fine, silver thread woven through to create intricate patterns that shimmered in the right light. Matching form-fitting trousers of the softest satin and black heeled boots that hugged his calves up to his knees.

Alexius, meanwhile, was dressed in more Solièrian style clothing. A crimson doublet with gold brocade, a high collar with a small ruff. A black cape pinned to one shoulder that fell down to his waist in gleaming velvet and trousers only a shade darker than his doublet, that showed off his well-muscled legs in a way that made it difficult for Jayce not to look at them.

Finally, they arrived at the Grand Duke's estate, and Jayce realised that if he thought the de Viccarri estate was impressive, it was nothing compared to the Grand Duke's.

The gardens seemed to go on for miles. Shrubberies that had been trimmed to resemble animals such as stags and panthers and even a drake breathing fire flanked the pathway that led their carriage up to the main courtyard.

And the house looked more like a palace, with ivory walls and towering turrets. The windows lit up amber with candlelight.

A footman greeted them at the front doors and led them inside. Jayce and Alexius were escorted into an expansive ballroom with arched ceilings and white walls awash in the golden light cast from the lit chandeliers. It was already filled with people in colourful and elaborate outfits. Music mingled with the voices echoing throughout the room.

A servant wearing a feathered hat announced their arrival. "His lordship, Sir Alexius Auguste de Viccarri, and accompanying him, Jayce Marken."

They were led through the crowd of partygoers to stand in front of the Grand Duke Edmond and his wife Duchess Yvette. They were a handsome couple, Jayce thought. The duke looked much the same as he had the first time Jayce had met him when he first arrived in Étoisaint; long black curls and a thin, black moustache, and wearing clothes that looked as if they would cost as much as a small house.

The duchess stood at the same height as her husband. Her pale blonde hair was done up in a complicated pile on the top of her head, adorned with small amber gemstones that matched the colour of her dress. Her face was powdered in white with a dusting of pink on her cheeks.

Once they'd given their greetings, Jayce and Alexius retreated into the crowd.

They had barely done so when a bell-like voice was heard, calling out, "Alexius!"

A young woman appeared from out of the surrounding throng of people to fling herself at Alexius. Jayce could tell straight away that she was the daughter of the duke and duchess. With her pale hair and crystal-clear blue eyes, she was the spitting image of the duchess. She wore a dress of gold material with black lacing, similar in fashion to Duchess Yvette's. Unlike the duchess, however, the young woman's dress showed off an ample amount of cleavage. Enough that Jayce had to make a conscious effort not to look anywhere below her neck.

"It's been so long since we last saw each other," the young woman said, clinging to Alexius's arm.

Alexius let out a good-natured laugh. "Apologies, Your Grace. I have been busy of late."

She pouted her painted lips. "Too busy for me?"

Ah, Jayce observed. *It's like that.*

"And who is your friend?" she asked, finally turning her attention to Jayce. "I do not believe we've met before?"

"Jayce Marken," said Jayce, taking the young lady's extended hand and placing a kiss upon it, as was custom. "I had the good fortune of running into Alexius at the Dark Citadel, and he's kindly allowed me to live under his roof for the time being."

"How kind. That sounds just like our Alexius."

"He certainly is a generous soul, our Alexius," said Jayce, seriously.

The young lady giggled. "And I am Marie, daughter of Duke Edmond and Duchess Yvette."

"Of course. You have your mother's beauty and your father's regal bearing."

Marie flushed pink. "Alexius, your companion is positively charming."

"He is, isn't he?"

Jayce raised a discreet brow, to which Alexius responded with a discreet wink.

"Oh, Alexius, come with me," said Marie, tugging on his arm.

"There's something I simply must show you. And you can tell me about everything that's happened since we last saw each other."

"If you say so. Jayce, are you coming?"

But Jayce was already shaking his head. "You go on," he said. "I'd like to find something to drink first."

Alexius looked suddenly worried. "Are you well?"

"Of course. Just a little parched is all."

"Alexius." Marie gave his arm another impatient tug. "Come along now."

"I'll find you later," he told Jayce before finally allowing Marie to lead him away, leaving Jayce behind.

Which was fine.

Alexius deserved to spend some time catching up with old friends without Jayce dogging his footsteps.

It didn't take long for him to find the buffet table. Long and draped in purple cloth, it held a wide assortment of mouth-watering dishes, such as poached pears sprinkled with sugar. Steaming bowls of onion soup, oysters, and scallops. Escargots, chicken braised with wine and garlic, steamed mussels in white wine sauce, and every type of cheese in existence, Jayce was sure.

The centrepiece was a huge ice sculpture, carved into the shape of a swan in flight that didn't appear to be in danger of melting any time soon.

Jayce reached for one of the glass goblets and poured himself some water from the silver carafe, forgoing the wines and ciders on offer.

"Well, well. I didn't expect to see you here tonight."

Jayce turned at the sound of the familiar voice to find none other than Florent. He had to admit that Florent looked positively striking in his party finery. His doublet was emerald green with puffed sleeves at the shoulders. His brown curls had been pulled back into a short ponytail and he wore the most imperceptible hint of red paint on his full lips. Whereas his eyes were lined thickly with black kohl, making his green irises appear more vivid.

"Florent," said Jayce. "I can't say I was expecting to see you here either."

"Then I can only hope seeing me has come as a pleasant surprise to you."

"That's what I should be saying."

Florent's smile grew more flirtatious. "Seeing you is always a pleasure."

Instead of responding, Jayce took another sip from his glass. What was he doing? He didn't mean to encourage Florent's advances, but at the same time, he couldn't help feeling a bit playful around the elf. Maybe a part of him just liked to pretend that it was Alexius who was flirting with him like this. Looking at him with such open admiration and desire.

Florent stepped forward to stand beside Jayce at the buffet table, reaching for his own glass and pouring himself some of the mulled wine.

"I'm assuming Alexius invited you? Where is he, by the way? I thought the two of you would be stuck to each other's sides."

"He was stolen away by the duke's daughter," Jayce said.

"Oh, Marie? That doesn't sound surprising. She's been in love with Alexius since she was a girl," mused Florent. "And she appears to have grown into exactly the type of woman that fits Alexius's preferences."

"Is that so?" Jayce kept his voice as neutral as possible. "And what preferences are those, exactly?"

"Classically beautiful," said Florent, as if he were reciting a list. "Blonde. Large breasts."

Ah. Most things Jayce was decidedly not.

"I see," was all he said, trying not to feel too oddly dejected.

"You know, I did try to invite Iris here tonight," Florent said.

"Oh? I'm guessing they turned you down?"

"They said, and I quote, 'I would rather sit on a hot stove with my breeches pulled down than attend a party for people so absurdly wealthy they probably shit in toilets made of gold.'"

Jayce couldn't stop the laugh that burst forth even if he tried.

"They have a way with words, that one," Florent chuckled.

"It must be all the time they spend around books. It's given them quite the lyrical vocabulary."

"Perhaps we can expect the same of you in time, now that you work in their bookstore and all?"

"Perhaps. One day, I might start speaking exclusively like I swallowed a book of poetry."

The music, which had been soft and blended into the background noise until now, suddenly changed its tune. Becoming louder and more exuberant. Jayce didn't need to see the crowd gathering in the middle of the ballroom floor before he realised a dance had started up.

Guests were pairing up to dance a classic Solièran dance, which started with the pair standing side by side, their joined hands held in the air between them while they took five measured steps forward, then three backward, before finally, they could put their arms around one another and begin the dance in earnest.

As Jayce watched each of the dancers make their way around the dance floor, he found himself caught off guard when he noticed Alexius among them. And of course, the one dancing with him was Marie, who looked incandescent with glee at being able to dance with the young de Viccarri knight. She was sure to be the envy of every eligible young woman here—and maybe some men.

As for Alexius, he seemed perfectly happy to be dancing with the duke's daughter. He had that endearingly wide smile on his face. The smile that brought out the dimples in his cheeks that Jayce had imagined kissing countless times.

Jayce also couldn't help but notice the way Alexius's gaze every now and again wandered down to the bosom that was pressed against his chest. Marie seemed to take notice of this, and rather than be offended, she smiled coyly and leaned closer to whisper something into Alexius's ear.

The smile on Alexius's face turned a touch coy as well.

Jayce's grip on his glass goblet grew tighter. An unpleasant feeling curdled in the pit of his stomach. It was similar to the one he had felt on the morning he had woken up to find Alexius and Katrina leaving the bathroom together.

"Jayce." The sound of Florent calling his name snapped his attention away from where Alexius and Marie were dancing. Florent was looking at him with a knowing smile, and Jayce wondered if he had truly been so obvious just now.

"I forgot to ask you," he said. "How did you like the book I sent you?"

"Oh. It was . . . a lovely gift. Thank you."

"And you saw the note I left inside it."

Jayce averted his eyes. "I did."

"Then I'm sure you understand what the purpose of such a gift was?"

"I do."

"Jayce, I—"

Florent's words were forestalled by two men, one human and one a golden scaled drakekin, with their arms around each other, both laughing, stumbled up to the buffet table. One of them almost bumped into Jayce.

"Whoops!" the drakekin proclaimed loudly but jovially. "Sorry, lads!"

"No problem at all, good sir," Florent said amicably, then much quieter to Jayce, "Let's find somewhere a bit more private to talk."

He followed Florent through the crowd and over to the base of the wide staircase that led into the ballroom. There, they found a secluded nook in between the staircase and the wall, that was partially covered by a large frond from a potted plant.

Florent didn't waste any time with preamble. "As I was about to say, I like to believe I have made my intentions clear to you by now, and . . . I would like to know what your answer is?"

"I—you've only known me for a few weeks, Florent."

"I know, but from the moment I first saw you, I couldn't help but be taken with you. Admittedly, your beauty drew me in first, but then I got to know you and found myself falling for you even more."

Jayce opened his mouth and closed it again, unsure of how to answer. When Florent lifted a hand to cup his cheek, Jayce held himself stone still. The touch was impossibly light, and he knew that if he wanted to move away, Florent would let him. Florent would not chase after him.

Jayce didn't move away.

"I see the way you look at Alexius," Florent continued. "But even so, I don't think I would forgive myself if I didn't take the opportunity to tell you exactly how I feel while I can. Jayce, I've truly fallen for you, and if you chose to be with me, I promise I would do everything in my power to make you happy. My gaze would never be swayed by another. You would never have to watch on forlornly while I pranced about with someone else. Because my heart would belong to you and you alone. For as long as you would have it."

Pretty words, Jayce thought. Pretty enough that he was almost tempted to accept them. To accept what Florent was offering him. Jayce wanted it, he realised with a little bit of a shock. He wanted that kind of love affair. He wanted to be loved fiercely and wholly, the way Florent had promised to love him, and he wanted to give that love in return.

Jayce lifted his own hand to cover the one Florent held against his cheek.

And gently removed it.

But he wanted to have that love with the person of his choosing. And there was only one he would choose.

"I'm sorry," Jayce murmured. "Truly. But I don't think I can be yours."

Florent closed his eyes, as if dealt a physical blow. It was a splinter in the heart to see the hurt flicker across Florent's face. Despite it all, he did care for Florent, and that was another small shock to him.

"I understand," Florent finally said, a small but pained smile on his lips.

Jayce didn't have anything else to say. He was still gripping Florent's hand in his, and with one last squeeze, he let go and walked away.

Jayce didn't really have a destination in mind as he weaved through the throng of guests. Their voices and their laughter loud in his ears. He ended up on the outskirts of where the dancers were just finishing up. The musicians playing their final notes.

It didn't take long for him to spot Alexius across the dance floor with Marie still in his arms.

They came to a halt, just as the music did. Jayce watched as Alexius and Marie bowed to each other, as the rest of the dancers did to their partners.

But then he saw the two of them do something that none of the other dancers did. As Alexius straightened up out of his bow, Marie threw herself back into his arms. Jayce imagined that beneath the hem of her gown, Marie was pushing herself up onto the tips of her toes so she could place a kiss at the corner of Alexius's mouth.

Alexius didn't push her away.

And Jayce didn't hang around to witness anymore of it.

As soon as Jayce was alone on the balcony, he let out a sigh of relief. The sounds of the music and the chatter from the ballroom inside faded to a soft drone as he pressed himself up against the marble railing. The duke's expansive gardens spread out below him.

Jayce focused on the sounds of the singing crickets in the garden, on the rushing of water from some fountain in the distance. On the cool night breeze, weaving through his hair and gliding along his cheeks.

He focused on anything that would put the thoughts of Alexius and Marie out of his mind. The way she clung to him and batted her pretty blonde eyelashes at him. The way she kissed him. And how Alexius didn't seem to mind any of it. Even seeming to enjoy the attention she was lavishing on him—

So much for not thinking about them.

Jayce heaved himself up onto the balcony railing until he was perched on it, with his boots dangling over the garden. If he tipped forward too much, he might fall. Plummet three storeys, and most likely sustain a serious injury or two.

I'm sure that would take my mind off of Alexius and his soon-to-be bed partner, he thought dryly.

He wished Alexius had never asked him to come here tonight. Why had Alexius even invited him? Jayce had barely seen him since they first walked through the doors.

"Jayce?"

Stunned, he peered over his shoulder to see none other than Alexius striding across the balcony towards him. The wind barely ruffled the stiff curls on his head.

"Alexius," said Jayce. "What are you doing out here?"

"I should be the one asking you that," Alexius said, coming to stand next to Jayce. "You shouldn't be sitting like that. You could fall."

Jayce was surprised by the comment, and also oddly touched by the concern. "It's fine. I'm not that clumsy, you know?"

"Still, it's dangerous."

"It's not the most dangerous thing I've ever done."

Alexius chuckled, taking a seat on the railing as well. "Go on then. Brag to me about all the death defying adventures you went on over the years."

"I would, but we might be here all night if I did, and I'd hate to keep you away from your charming little companion."

"Marie?"

"Yes. I'm sure you'll have little trouble wooing her into your bed tonight."

Alexius looked as if Jayce had just slapped him across the face. "What the fuck, Jayce? Why would I want—why would you say that?"

"What? Is that not what you want?"

"Of course not!"

"Well, it's certainly what she wants."

"I don't give a damn." Alexius raked an agitated hand through his hair. "Gods."

Jayce scowled. "Forgive me for seeing the way you acted with one another and making an assumption."

"What do you mean, the way I acted with her?" demanded Alexius. "Do you mean that I danced with her?"

"Don't be obtuse. I saw her kiss you. And even before then, she was clearly interested in you."

"What would you have had me do? Push her away and cause a scene and offend her and her parents? I was just trying to be polite!"

Jayce cocked an eyebrow at him. "Oh, yes, you were being very polite when you were staring at her cleavage."

"I didn't *stare* at her cleavage. I just . . ." Alexius made a disgruntled sound. "I couldn't *not* look at it for just a brief moment when she was . . . so very close, is all."

Jayce only scoffed and rolled his eyes.

"Why are we even arguing about this?" said Alexius after a pause. Then, when Jayce did not reply, "I *don't* want to sleep with Marie, by the way."

"It's not as if I'd care if you did," Jayce said with a shrug.

"Wouldn't you?"

He gave Alexius a sharp look. "What are you trying to say?"

"Nothing. Nothing." Another pause. "Well, what about you and Florent, then?"

"Again, what are you trying to say?"

"Just that he seems to be around you a lot these days and . . . I see the way he looks at you."

"How does he look at me?" Jayce asked, feigning ignorance.

"Like he wants to bed you," said Alexius, clearly not in the mood for dancing around with words. "And I hope that you're being careful around him."

Jayce let out a mirthless laugh. "Rest assured, Alexius, I'm more than capable of defending myself from the advances of lustful men.

Unless I want them, of course."

"And do you? Want Florent's advances, that is?"

Jayce thought about saying yes, just to toy with Alexius. To see what sort of reaction that might elicit from him. Would it make him jealous? The way Jayce had felt while watching him with other women, like Marie and Katrina? Or would he simply slap Jayce on the back with a grin and wish him good luck?

Jayce wasn't sure he was in the mood to listen to Alexius being encouraging of him fucking another man. "No. Unfortunately for Florent, there's only one man I really want."

Oh no. No, he hadn't meant to say that last part.

"And who's that?" Alexius demanded.

Jayce thought he might have heard some heat behind Alexius's words, but when he looked at him, the other man's expression was calm.

"I . . ." he started and paused.

It would be so easy to put forth any name. Even a made up one. But the last thing Jayce wanted was to spin a web of lies that he would inevitably get tangled up in. *Oh well, might as well get this over with.*

Angling his body so he could face Alexius properly and look him square in the eyes, he said, "You, Alexius. I would actually appreciate *your* advances because it seems that I've fallen in love with you."

Silence. Alexius's expression had morphed from calm curiosity to confusion to a slow-dawning comprehension before finally settling on looking like a fish out of water, eyes wide and mouth hanging open.

Jayce hoped it didn't show on his face, the twinge of hurt he felt that Alexius had yet to say anything and was only staring at him like Jayce was some odd creature.

He cleared his throat. "Right, well." Jayce swung his legs around until he could plant his feet on the white stone balcony floor. He stood and began to move away. "I think I might head home now."

"Wait, Jayce." Alexius reached out to grab his hand, and Jayce instinctively tried to jerk away, but Alexius held fast. "You can't say something like that to me and just *leave*."

"You weren't saying anything."

"I was surprised I—Hold on, come with me."

Jayce allowed Alexius to lead him over to a more secluded part of the massive balcony. Out of the view from the ballroom glass doors and under the cover of one of the overreaching trees by the wall.

However, Jayce certainly hadn't expected Alexius to press him up against the wall and cage him in with his hands pressed to the wall on either side of Jayce's head in one swift movement. Jayce would never admit to how being in this position—with Alexius leaning in close to him and looking at him with such intensity to his dark eyes—made his heart dance a frantic number in his chest.

"And you can't say something like that to me all of a sudden and not expect me to be lost for words," said Alexius, his voice low and husky.

Jayce tilted his head. "Speaking isn't always needed to convey how one thinks or feels. Sometimes silence speaks for itself."

For a moment, Alexius looked as if Jayce's words had stumped him before he hung his head in helpless laughter.

When he returned his gaze to Jayce, his expression was warm. "All right then," he said. "Will you give me another chance? Will you allow me to say what I would've liked to say had the cogs in my head not stopped turning momentarily?"

"If you must," Jayce tried to say as flippantly as possible, but the words came out sounding half strangled.

"Good. But first, you have to say it again."

"Say what?"

"You know what. Don't tell me you're going to be stubborn about it now? Or should I say cowardly?"

Jayce gritted his teeth, the word rankling him. Lifting his chin and looking Alexius in the eye as he did last time, Jayce said,

"I've fallen in love with you, Alexius de Viccarri. So much so that I fear I may end up striking the next woman to show her cleavage to you."

A giddy laugh erupted from Alexius's lips. He was smiling so broadly and unabashedly, in a way that made his face light up so brightly, Jayce almost found it difficult to look directly at him.

"Are you going to give me a response this time or not?" Jayce asked when all Alexius continued to do was laugh.

"Right. Of course," Alexius said around the laughter.

Composing himself, Alexius leaned in close, so close Jayce thought for a moment that Alexius was about to kiss him, and he felt his heart stutter. But the press of lips against lips never came. Instead, Alexius moved until his mouth was close to Jayce's ear. So Jayce could feel the warmth of Alexius's breath against a surprisingly sensitive patch of his skin.

And then Alexius spoke, the words barely more than a whisper, but with him so close, Jayce heard it as clear as day.

"I love you, too."

Now it was Jayce's turn to be at a loss for words.

Alexius pulled back so they could look at each other once more and the way he looked at Jayce felt like a punch to the chest. It made him wonder how he could have been so stupid to not notice Alexius's feelings before. If Alexius had been looking at him like that this whole time.

"H-How long?"

One of Alexius's hands left their position on the wall by Jayce's head to cradle the curve of his jaw instead. A thumb rubbing softly at the skin there. Jayce didn't bother to hide the shiver this elicited.

"Long enough," said Alexius. "Long enough that I am . . . *desperate* to kiss you right now. If you'll allow me to?"

His thumb had shifted to stroking just below Jayce's lower lip. The barely there touch of Alexius's blunt thumb nail against his lip was unbearable.

Jayce's voice appeared to have abandoned him for the time being, so all he could do was nod his permission. He had the satisfaction of seeing Alexius's gaze darken before he swooped in to claim Jayce's mouth with his own.

The kiss wasn't hard or fuelled by desperation the way Jayce might have thought it would be. Instead, it was a gentle thing. At first, it was barely more than a brushing of lips, before Alexius decided to deepen it just so.

The chasteness of it didn't make it any less breath-taking, however.

Alexius's fingers threaded gently through his hair and Jayce thought such a tender touch coupled with such a tender kiss might be his undoing.

Just as he had been the one to initiate the kiss, Alexius was the one to end it. When he pulled away, he remained close enough that Jayce could still feel his breath.

"You have no idea just how long I've wanted to do that," Alexius said, his voice heavy with desire.

Jayce fisted the front of Alexius's brocade, pulling him in closer. "Kiss me again," he demanded against Alexius's mouth. "I need—"

He never had to finish the rest of his sentence, for it seemed that Alexius was just as keen to have his mouth back on Jayce's.

The kiss, this time, was heavier than the last, more insistent. As if the feelings they had both been keeping bottled up were finally starting to spill forth.

Jayce's hands wandered from their grip on Alexius's doublet and up to the strong shape of his jaw. He cradled the clean-shaven skin there, as well using it to coax the knight into deepening their kiss even further.

Alexius groaned, almost piteously, when Jayce bit down lightly, teasingly, on his lip. Jayce, in turn, let out a pleasantly startled sound when one of Alexius's muscled arms snaked around the back of his waist, while the other reached up to cradle the back of Jayce's head. No longer was Jayce pressed against the wall. Now he was pressed against Alexius's body.

He could feel the heat of him beneath his luxuriously tailored clothes. And the hard planes and curves of Alexius's exquisite musculature flush against his own body.

And his muscles certainly weren't the only hard thing Jayce could feel pressing against him.

Once more, Alexius was the one to end their kiss, doing so when he seemed to become fully aware of his own body's reaction.

"I-I'm sorry," he stammered out, looking mortified with himself. "I don't normally—This isn't to say I'm expecting—"

Hopelessly endeared, Jayce hushed him with a finger to his lips. With a mischievous curl of his lips, Jayce said, "Perhaps another time."

Alexius's own mouth lifted into a grin.

Then they were both laughing.

Helpless and affectionate.

Chapter
Fourteen

Jayce thought that Alexius had done a rather admirable job of keeping his affections for him a complete secret until now.

After the Grand Duke's party, however, it seemed that something had cracked in Alexius, and he could no longer keep his feelings to himself. He took any and every opportunity that he could to be close to Jayce. To touch him and to kiss him. If he found Jayce curled up on the couch reading, he would wander over, only to press his lips to Jayce's forehead. If Alexius got up in the mornings to find Jayce already in the dining room, enjoying his breakfast, then he would greet him with an arm around his shoulders and a tender kiss either to Jayce's lips, or cheek or even the back of his hand. Completely uncaring about whether Estelle or any of the other house staff were present. If any of the staff were surprised by this new relationship between Jayce and Alexius, they did not show it.

Alexius never took anything further than a kiss or a gentle touch. Which was fine at first, but after a while, Jayce began to think he would not mind if it led to something more carnal.

He almost thought it would when one day, Alexius came to visit Jayce while he was working, and somehow, they had ended up with

Jayce pressed against a shelf, with Alexius's mouth hot and instant against his. Alexius's body a hard and heavy—but welcome—weight against him. Sadly, it had ended with them being interrupted by an unimpressed Iris carrying a very judgemental-looking Fable.

"Not during working hours, if you please," they had said. "And not against the books."

Properly mortified, he and Alexius agreed to keep those sorts of activities out of the bookshop.

For the next few weeks, Jayce was happier than he had ever been—than he thought he would ever be. He'd heard the way people described a new love in books and in ballads and was almost shocked to find that it was all true. Being with Alexius, loving Alexius and being loved by Alexius was more euphoric and intoxicating than he ever could have predicted it to be.

Jayce knew he had been in love with Alexius for a long time now and had grown accustomed to those feelings some time ago. But now, knowing that Alexius loved him back was something completely different.

Sometimes it felt as if it were too good to be true.

Sometimes it felt like he didn't deserve such goodness in his life.

He kept those thoughts tucked away in a private corner of himself. If only for the sake of Alexius's happiness.

Jayce thought there were no lengths he would not go to to keep that gorgeous smile on Alexius's face.

~

"You know," Jayce said while he and Alexius sat in the de Viccarri estate's gardens, beneath the shade of the peach tree. "There was a while there where I thought your tastes ran exclusively towards women."

Alexius looked up at him. He was resting on his back and with his head in Jayce's lap. "And what changed that assumption?" he asked.

"When I caught you looking at that book with the drawing of a man having his cock sucked."

With a heavy sigh, Alexius pressed a palm to his forehead. "Are you ever going to let me forget that?"

"That remains to be seen."

"You are right, though. I've always liked both men and women. Joséphine was my first, but after she and I ended things, there was a time where I had dalliances with a few men, too. But it's been a long time now since there was anyone I was serious about. Until you."

Jayce plucked at one of Alexius's curls. "Is that supposed to make me feel special?"

"I hope I always make you feel special."

"Aren't you a charmer?"

"Only for you." Alexius flashed him a grin. Then, more seriously, "And you? What is your preference?"

Jayce tilted his head up to the branches arcing above them, squinting at the glimmers of sunlight that winked through the gaps. "It's not something I've ever really stopped to consider before. But I can't imagine discriminating either."

They lapsed into comfortable silence for a while. The leaves rustled softly in the breeze, the birds sang to one another, and Alexius closed his eyes and hummed contently every now and again, as Jayce lightly combed his fingers through his hair.

Their moment of tranquillity alone together was interrupted by Estelle's approach.

"Pardon me," she said, severe as ever. "But this letter just arrived for you, Alexius."

She handed him a cream envelope with a red wax seal.

"Thank you, Estelle," said Alexius and once she left, he broke the seal and pulled out a folded letter.

Jayce was content to give Alexius privacy to read his letter. But after a reasonable amount of time had gone by and Alexius still had yet to look up from the letter, Jayce grew concerned.

"Alexius?" he asked gently. "Is everything all right?"

That seemed to snap Alexius out of whatever reverie he had gotten himself into. "Yes," he said turning to face Jayce. "Yes, everything is fine. It's just . . ." He reached out to take one of Jayce's hands. "Jayce, I have something to tell you."

"What is it? You're not leaving me for another lover already, are you?"

"No. Not yet," he joked with a small smile. "I probably should have told you this sooner, but I—I didn't want to get your hopes up in case nothing eventuated."

Jayce tightened his fingers around Alexius's. "Alexius, what are you saying?"

His lover took a deep breath, as if steeling himself for what he was about to say next. "We found your mother."

It took some time for the words to sink in and once they did, they had a devastating effect. Jayce slipped his hand from Alexius's. He didn't know what he was feeling in that moment. His thoughts felt too muddled and his emotions too overwhelming.

"I—You found her?" Jayce swallowed. Words were clogging up his throat. "How—When did—"

Alexius, apparently taking pity on Jayce, started to explain. "It was not long after we arrived in Étoisaint. I . . . decided to ask a favour of the Grand Duke. I told him that I wanted to help reunite you with your mother, if she was still alive, but that you had little memory of her. You only remembered that she lived on an apple orchard. He agreed to help, even though it was a near impossible task, which is why I didn't want to tell you in the first place, in case it turned out that she couldn't be found."

"And—And where is she?"

"She's in Ponfier. On an apple orchard."

Ponfier. He knew the name. A town near the northern coast of Solière. Was that where he had called home before he was stolen?

Jayce's eyes drifted to the letter in Alexius's hand and his breath caught. "Is that—?"

"No," Alexius assured, immediately catching his meaning. "No, this is from the duke. I asked him that if they found her, they not tell her about you in the event that she come racing here straight away and give you the fright of your life."

"But if you didn't—How do you even know it's her?"

Again, Alexius paused before he shuffled the letter in his hand, pulling out a second piece of parchment and handed it to Jayce.

He felt the breath leave him once more.

Looking up at him from the paper in his hands was a miniature pencil portrait of a woman. Round face framed by a curtain of dark-coloured hair. She had a sweet face with lines around her eyes and mouth that led Jayce to believe she was on the cusp of her later years. She was also instantly familiar to him because—

"She looks like you," Alexius's voice came out in a whisper.

Jayce's throat felt thick with emotion. There was no doubt this was the face of his mother. After all these years, he could finally remember what she looked like. And now he knew where to find her, too. What would she do when she saw him? What would she think? Most importantly, what would she think of him when she found out where he had been and what he had been doing all these years?

When Jayce finally found his voice again, he said, "I—I can't see her again. Not right now. I need some time."

"Of course," Alexius said. "Take all the time you need . . . and I'm sorry for not telling you about this."

Jayce shook his head. "No, you have nothing to apologise for. If anything, I should be thanking you. I'm not even sure I ever would have been able to work up the courage to try and find her myself."

Alexius held his arms out, and Jayce allowed himself to fall into the embrace.

The idea of meeting his mother again was exciting and terrifying all at once. He had no idea how she would react to him and the awful things he had done as Grey. But Jayce reminded himself that no matter what happened, he would be able to come back to someone who knew of the worst parts of him and chose to love him, regardless.

Chapter
Fifteen

With the first day of summer came the preparations for the Knights Tourney.

The Knights Tourney was a well-loved tradition in Solière, the first ever Tourney dating back more than a hundred years ago. It was supposed to take place every two years, but this year would be the first time the Knights Tourney would occur since the start of the Dark Lord's war.

"What better way to celebrate the end of the war," the Grand Duke had said when he first made the announcement in the town square, "Than with the return of this land's oldest and most beloved of games?"

The Knights Tourney was coming back to Solière, and it was being hosted in Étoisaint.

Before long, visitors from all across Solière were arriving in Étoisaint, ready to bear witness to the Tourney that would not even begin for another fortnight. Soon, the town was bustling with even more people than usual.

And it was not just eager spectators flocking to Étoisaint for the Tourney, but knights too. All intent on competing. All intent on being crowned a Tourney Champion.

Giving the competition its name, only knights could enter the Tourney. It was made up of three games: horse racing, sword duels, and jousting.

Even though Jayce could not be any more disinterested in sports, he found he was looking forward to the Tourney. He had never seen one, after all.

But he'd be lying if he said that was the only reason he was looking forward to the Tourney.

For the next fortnight, Alexius was swept up in training for the impending Tourney. He would be competing in the duels.

One bright afternoon, Alexius was practicing some sword work in the horses' pasture while Jayce read under the shade of a nearby tree. Blackfire and the piebald mare Jayce had since named Léa were grazing further down the pasture. Uncaring of the antics of their humans.

At one point, Jayce paused in his reading to watch Alexius execute a couple of complex sword thrusts and parries.

He had excellent form, Jayce thought. Although that was no surprise. His movements were powerful yet graceful. Even simply by watching him train, it was easy to see how Alexius had come to be knighted, and at such a young age.

"You aren't just trying to impress me, are you?" Jayce asked once Alexius had finished the set he'd been working through.

Alexius turned to face him. His skin was sheened with sweat and his chest and shoulders rose and fell heavily beneath his shirt. He grinned lazily. "That depends. Is it working?"

Jayce closed the book and set it aside. "Maybe," he said, rising so he could come out from under the shelter of the tree and stand before Alexius.

"Only maybe? I guess I'll have to try even harder," said Alexius. "After all, I'd hate to make a fool of myself in front of you at the Tourney."

"In front of me? What about all the hundreds of other people who will be there to watch and spread the tale of your epic failure to all corners of the land?"

"I don't care about whether I impress them or not. The only one I want to make sure I look good in front of is you."

Jayce tried—and failed—to keep the pleased smile off his face. "Not even Marie?"

"Not even Marie."

"Or what about that other woman you brought over that first morning I was here? Katrina, was it?"

Alexius dropped his head and let out a long-suffering sigh. "I said, no one except for you. Now go back to your reading, you devil. You're distracting me."

He determinedly resumed his training stance. Before he could start fighting off his invisible opponents, Jayce put a hand on Alexius's lightly stubbled cheek, turning it to face him.

"That wasn't me trying to distract you." He leaned up and delivered a slow, deep kiss to Alexius's lips.

The kiss went on for some time and Jayce felt the tension bleed out of Alexius. Felt the way the other man became attuned only to Jayce and the meeting of their lips.

Only when he knew for sure that every part of Alexius was focused solely and irrevocably on him did Jayce pull away. He enjoyed the slightly dazed look on Alexius's face and the way he tried momentarily to chase the kiss.

With a smile Jayce said, "That was."

"Huh?" Alexius uttered ineloquently.

But Jayce was already turning away, leaving Alexius to return to his spot beneath the tree.

One of the horses whinnied in the distance.

~

"All this time and effort and money spent on one day of watching a group of armoured meat-heads swing swords at each other and try to knock each other down with large sticks," Iris said contemptuously.

"Careful, Iris," said Florent. "I happen to be one of those armoured meat-heads."

Iris looked unfazed. "I stand by what I said."

Along with Iris and Florent, Jayce was sitting on a grassy hill overlooking where the stands for the Knights Tourney were being erected outside of the town.

It was a pleasant afternoon and Florent had invited Jayce and Iris to join him on a little impromptu picnic while they took a break from the shop.

"If you're in the Tourney, how come you aren't training, Florent?" Jayce asked the elf, as he reached for the platter of fruits, crackers and cheeses laid out between them. He plucked himself a grape.

"I have been training, thank you very much," Florent replied haughtily. "Quite hard, in fact. But you can't expect me to kill myself training every second of every day. I need a break every once in a while."

"Alexius doesn't seem to have that mindset." The words came out more petulant than Jayce had intended.

Iris smirked. "Is someone feeling a bit lonely?"

Jayce resisted the urge to pelt the orc with a grape.

"If you are Jayce, you could always come spend some time with me?" said Florent, and with a wink, he added, "I'm always willing to make time for you."

Jayce did throw a grape at Florent.

Florent had indeed remained friendly with Jayce, even after the ball, and he'd shown no sort of ill will when he found out that Jayce had started going out with Alexius. Occasionally, he made suggestive remarks such as this, but it was in jest—at least, Jayce hoped it was.

"This would be Alexius's first time competing in the Tourney," Iris remarked. "So, it's not surprising to hear that he's so determined."

"It is my first time, too," Florent added.

"Yes, but I think being in the Knights Tourney means more to him than it does to you. Don't pretend that being in the Tourney isn't just about showing off for you."

Florent didn't dispute it, nor did he look particularly perturbed by Iris's statement.

"Do you know what competitions he's taking part in?" Iris asked Jayce.

"The duels," said Jayce.

To Florent this time. "And you?"

"Duels and racing," said Florent.

"No jousting?" asked Jayce.

"Only veterans enter the jousting. It's even more dangerous than the duels."

Jayce frowned. "What do you mean, even more dangerous?"

"Apart from the races," Iris began, "all the games have some element of danger to them. No knight is allowed to kill another, or to even purposefully try to injure each other. But sometimes accidents happen."

"Surely it can't be any more dangerous than fighting in a war," said Jayce.

"Definitely not," Florent said. "But knights have still been known to walk away from the Tourney with serious injuries."

"I've even heard of a knight who was stabbed in the eye," Iris said. They must have seen the look on Jayce's face because they quickly added, "They survived, though."

But Jayce found that did little to quell the new worry bubbling like a boiling soup inside of him.

He looked out to the stands being built in the distance and thought that maybe now he felt some of the contempt Iris had had when he looked at them.

~

It was nearing sundown and Jayce was walking through the streets on his way home after a day's work.

Home.

He wasn't sure when he had come to think of Alexius's estate as such, and it came as a bit of a shock to him every time he caught himself thinking of it that way.

Jayce cut through the town square as the bell tower chimed the hour. There he noticed a woman standing in front of the noticeboard. She was wearing leathers and her hair was as black as a raven's feather and fell all the way down to the backs of her knees in a single braid. She was also in possession of a long, pointed tail that was a deep plum colour, and two horns that curled out from the front of her forehead and over her scalp. A shadeborn.

Detlas's wanted poster was still there, the paper now showing signs of weathering. On the available space beside it, the shadeborn was putting up her own poster.

"'Join the reformed Mercenaries Guild'." Jayce read aloud as he came to stand beside the woman. "I'm not sure the duke would appreciate you trying to recruit killers for hire in his town."

She turned to him with a friendly smile. She had a scar on her chin, and she was at least a head taller than him. "Like the poster says, we're *reformed*. Think of the Mercenaries Guild as more like . . . helpers for hire these days."

"Helpers for hire?" Jayce arched an eyebrow. "What? Are you going to scrub toilets and hang washing for a handful of coins?"

The shadeborn belted out a hearty laugh. A few passersby cast her strange looks.

"You're a funny one. I like that. But no. Towns like this one have been lucky not to feel the brunt of the war. But there are plenty of places and plenty of people who have. Who have been left vulnerable because of it. And plenty who will look to use that vulnerability as an opportunity. Our goal is to provide aid to everyone and anyone who needs it."

"If many of these people are in as dire straits as you say," said

Jayce, "then what happens if they don't have the coin to afford your protection?"

"It's not a matter of coin to us," the shadeborn said. "They can pay us as much or as little as they can afford. And if they cannot pay us at all, then we will wait to collect until the day they can. Are you thinking about joining up?"

Jayce did not answer right away. He stared at the poster with its bold, black lettering.

"Our goal is to provide aid to everyone and anyone who needs it."

Alexius once told him that he should try to atone for the atrocities of his past. Maybe this was how he could do just that? After all the years he helped bring despair and destruction to Solière, this could be how he helped to make it a better place, even if only a little bit.

But joining this Mercenaries Guild would mean leaving Étoisaint.

It would mean leaving Alexius.

And yet . . .

"I'll . . . need to think it over," Jayce said.

"I understand," said the shadeborn. "Should you come to a decision, I'll be staying at the inn here for the next few days. After that I head back to the Crown City. The name's Latasha, by the way."

She took her leave, leaving Jayce standing before the noticeboard with his head and his heart feeling like a jumbled mess.

~

"Why are you looking forward to being in this Tourney so much?"

They were in Alexius's bedroom, with Jayce sitting on the edge of his bed while Alexius changed out of his armour and into something more comfortable for dinner.

"Why do you ask that?" Alexius said, doing up the belt around his trousers.

Jayce shrugged. "I was curious. It seems to me that most knights enter the Tourney for the fame and glory that comes with it. But you already have quite enough of that. And even so, you're not the type to care too much about such things."

Alexius looked as if he were seriously contemplating his answer. "I suppose . . . because it seems like fun."

"Fun? You think competing in games that could maim you seems like fun?"

"There's always an element of risk when it comes to sports like these," Alexius said. "But I wouldn't say the chances of being injured for life are *that* high."

"There's still the chance, though," Jayce pointed out. "You just survived a war, and without any serious injury. Do you really want to risk it now just for some tournament?"

Alexius paused, and for a moment, Jayce thought he might have stepped out of line, and that now Alexius was angry with him.

Instead, the expression on Alexius's face when he looked at him was . . . delighted.

"Jayce," he said. "Are you worried about me?"

A warm flush rose to Jayce's cheeks. "I—So what if I am?"

Alexius came forward, took Jayce's head in his hands, and kissed him hard. Then, without breaking the kiss, he pushed forward until Jayce was lying flat on the bed with Alexius hovering over him. When he pulled away, Jayce had the ridiculous thought that Alexius looked like a child who had just been promised a second helping of dessert.

"What are you smiling about?" Jayce reached up to pinch lightly at Alexius's cheek, making his smile seem even wider.

"You care about me." Alexius said it as if that fact brought him infinite happiness.

"Yes. I believe that's been established."

Another kiss. This time, softer and lingering. It stayed as nothing more than a press of lips. Regardless of their position and where they were, Alexius never once took the opportunity to take things further. Even when Jayce put a hand to the back of Alexius's neck, pulling him in deeper so the kiss became more open-mouthed. Even when he thought he was giving some clear signs that he wanted *more*.

I may end up leaving to join the Mercenaries Guild, so please just take me now! He cried out in his head.

Still, Alexius's hands stayed where they were, braced on the blankets on either side of Jayce's head. An agonising space between their bodies.

Finally, the kiss came to an end, and they were looking into each other's faces once more. Alexius's expression was tender. As was his thumb stroking the skin of Jayce's temple.

"Don't worry," he murmured. "I'll come out of the Tourney in one piece."

A quick peck to Jayce's forehead, and then he was getting up.

Jayce was left feeling more than a little disappointed.

It appeared he would have to be more forward if he was going to get what he wanted.

Chapter
Sixteen

It was late into the night when Jayce left his bedroom.

He hadn't slept a wink and had spent the past few hours alternating between reading and staring into space, wondering.

Finally, he'd made up his mind and found himself walking down the darkened hallway. His heart beat faster with every step he took towards his destination, and reached a crescendo when he came to stand before a closed, oak door.

Jayce took a calming breath. He did not have to fear this. There was no reason to. Not if it was with Alexius.

He knocked softly on the door.

There was a long pause in which Jayce almost reconsidered this whole idea and was only a heartbeat away from flinging himself back down the hall and disappearing into his bedroom when the door opened.

"Jayce?" said Alexius. He was frowning at him as if he couldn't yet decide whether Jayce was really standing before him or not. "What are you doing here? It's late. I was having a really good dream actu—"

"Do you still want me?"

Alexius blinked. "What?"

"Do you still want me? Desire me? Wish to fuck me?"

"I—hang on. Come in, would you?"

He let Alexius take him by the wrist and gently tug him into his room.

"What's brought this on? And so late at night, too?"

"It's a yes or no question, de Viccarri," said Jayce. "Do you want me?"

"Yes," Alexius said, as if any other answer was inconceivable. "I still want you. Fuck, I'm not sure I could ever stop wanting you. But I wasn't sure whether that was something *you* wanted right now."

"It is." Exhilaration and perhaps even relief flooded through Jayce. It took everything in him to keep himself from grinning like a love-struck fool. "All right then, if you still want me, prove it. Fuck me right now."

Alexius's jaw fell open. "Now?"

"Unless what you just said now was all lies."

"Of course not. It's just that—Are you sure?"

"I would not be standing here now if I wasn't."

That seemed to be all it took to eliminate the vestiges of Alexius's hesitation. He surged forward, taking Jayce's face in his large palms, and delivered a bruising kiss.

Gripping the front of Alexius's nightshirt, Jayce pressed back just as insistently. Just as eagerly. He was so absorbed in the kiss, in the feel of Alexius's lips moving against his own and Alexius's calloused palms moving from his cheeks to stroke at the curve of his neck, that he hadn't even realised Alexius had manoeuvred them towards his bed until the backs of Jayce's legs hit the edge of the mattress.

Jayce fell back willingly onto the rumpled blankets. Willingly allowed Alexius to hover above him. Distantly, Jayce thought if someone had told him a year ago that he would allow another to put him in this position, he would have scoffed. Might have even felt revulsion at the thought of it. But he had not known Alexius then. Had not known the warmth of his presence or the way a smile from him could make Jayce feel as if there were dozens of butterflies flitting about in his stomach.

He had not known how even the lightest, most innocent touch from Alexius could make him feel like he could be someone to be cherished. Someone worthy of love.

Alexius pulled away and gazed down at Jayce with darkened eyes. Filled not only with lust, but something else. Affection maybe? Reverence?

Alexius's fingers trailed gently along the tops of Jayce's cheekbone. "Beautiful," Alexius murmured, and, oh, yes, that definitely sounded like reverence in his voice.

He should probably have said something in return. Something about how Alexius was the most gorgeous man Jayce had ever had the good fortune of laying eyes upon. How lucky Jayce felt to have his attention. His affection.

However, Jayce could not bring himself to vocalise his thoughts. Especially not when Alexius started trailing light kisses along his neck. All Jayce could bring himself to do was to arch into the ministrations and release a soft sigh. A hint of tongue licked at the scarring there. Jayce trembled.

It wasn't long before they both began to grow impatient. The need to feel more of the other's skin rising like the swelling of a wave. It didn't take long to rid Alexius of his loose nightshirt and undergarments. Jayce would have liked to have taken more time to appreciate the expanse of rich, dark skin across artfully sculpted musculature, on display before him. Alexius, however, was too preoccupied with getting Jayce out of his clothing.

When he was finally laid bare, Alexius looked at him as if he were a revelation. As if he were the most stunning creature he had ever seen, and Jayce felt a rush of embarrassment and the urge to cover himself up.

That was all forgotten once Alexius kissed him and started skating his hands slowly and gently across Jayce's body.

"You're so gorgeous," Alexius whispered against his collarbone.

"The most beautiful person I've ever seen."

Jayce swallowed. "Don't—Don't say those things."

Alexius lifted his head to fix him with a concerned look. "You don't like it?"

"I don't . . . any other time I-I don't mind. But not here. Not when we're—not like this—"

"All right, I won't say it anymore." He placed a hand against Jayce's cheek. "Are you okay? Do you still want to do this?"

Jayce nodded. Gods, he wanted it so badly. He did not think he'd be able to survive the night if they were to stop now.

Thankfully, Alexius did not need any further convincing. He resumed his exploration of Jayce's body with his mouth. Placing a kiss to his shoulder, chest, stomach. His thighs and ankle bones. He kept his touches light, as if Jayce were some sort of delicate porcelain that might crack with the wrong handling.

Jayce could not say he was as delicate. He couldn't keep himself from grabbing at the firm muscles of Alexius's behind while their hips were aligned. Or raking his nails down his back when Alexius bit at his clavicle. Tugging at the tufted curls on Alexius's head while he had Jayce's cock in his mouth.

Not that Alexius seemed to mind. In fact, where Jayce preferred tenderness, Alexius seemed to respond to a bit of roughness. Groaning and rolling his hips every time Jayce touched or kissed him with even a hint of force.

The hesitancies Jayce had managed to forget about until now reared their head when Alexius positioned his hips purposefully between Jayce's thighs.

They were both breathing heavily. The air felt overly warm and silvery light spilling in from outside showed off the sheen of perspiration on Alexius's skin. He looked magnificent.

"Is this all right?" Alexius's voice was husky and thick with want. He was so clearly on the very edge and yet, he was still asking Jayce what he wanted. Giving Jayce full control to put a halt to all this if he chose to.

Warmth that had nothing to do with the sex bloomed in his chest. Jayce nodded his head. "Fuck me."

So Alexius did.

He went slow. Jayce felt like he was shattering apart. He could not hold back the sounds clawing up from his throat. It seemed that Alexius couldn't either.

"*Gods*," Alexius breathed. His eyes squeezed shut and his head hung low so his lips hovered scant inches above Jayce's. "You are . . . you are incredible. Jayce. *Jayce*."

Jayce hadn't thought it would be like this. So intense and bright and wonderful. He hadn't been prepared. Not for how much he would enjoy it, and certainly not for the way he felt when he looked up at the man above him. Such a heady mix of desire and *love*.

Love.

He watched Alexius come apart.

I love him, he thought, as he pulled Alexius in for another kiss. Deep and slow.

I love him.

~

When Jayce next awoke, morning light filtering in through the tall window lit up the room with a golden hue.

Alexius lay beside him on the bed, still in a deep and sound sleep. Propping himself up on one elbow, Jayce decided to take the opportunity to observe the knight at his most unguarded. Lined in dusky gold, Alexius lay half on his side and half on his back, the twisted linen sheets just barely covering his modesty. His lips were parted, and Jayce had the urge to run his finger along his plush, lower lip, shaped like a bow. Trace the crease in the middle with the tip of his fingernail.

Happiness bloomed in Jayce's chest, bright and almost overwhelming, at being here with Alexius and getting to have this with Alexius. At the thought of what happened between the two of them last night and how it was so much better than Jayce could have possibly imagined it.

He could still feel the places on his body where Alexius had held him and touched him. Kissed him. Licked him. Some places were even a bit sore, but Jayce had to admit he liked it. Even if it did twinge when he shifted, it was only the faintest whisper of pain. It was proof that Alexius had been as gentle as could be, and it made Jayce's heart sing to think that he was important enough to Alexius that he would treat him with nothing less.

It wasn't long before Alexius made a sleepy sound and Jayce had the delight of watching him come awake.

He blinked around blearily at first, a small furrow between his brows. But when his eyes landed on Jayce, a pleased smile lit up his face.

"I was almost afraid I had dreamt you," he whispered, drowsily lifting a hand so he could trace a line down the side of Jayce's face with his fingertip.

In response, Jayce leaned down to kiss him. When he broke the kiss, pulling only far back enough that he could look upon Alexius's face, he asked, "Did that feel real enough to you?"

Looking more awake now, Alexius grinned. "You may have to do that one more time for me to be sure."

Jayce was only too happy to comply.

It was not long before their kissing turned into something else, with Alexius rolling on top of him, blanketing Jayce's body with his own, just as he had last night. Hands began to wander. Sighs and moans emitted from their mouths. Alexius groaned in a way that Jayce found all too pleasing when he hitched his legs up around the other man's waist.

Some long minutes later, the sun had fully risen in the sky and Jayce and Alexius lay tangled together on newly messed sheets. Now covered in sweat and both trying to regain their breaths. The turquoise blanket had since fallen completely off the bed, along with a couple of pillows.

Jayce lay with his head on Alexius's chest, enjoying the way it rose and fell rapidly and the sound of his thunderous heart beating almost in time with Jayce's own.

Alexius's fingers were slowly carding through his hair and in that moment, Jayce felt he would be content to never move from this position.

"I never thought I'd be able to have something like this," Jayce murmured, watching his own fingers as they traced idle patterns along Alexius's chest.

"Like this?" asked Alexius.

Jayce hesitated before answering. "A love like this."

He felt Alexius go still beneath him, clearly caught by surprise by Jayce's words.

Then, Alexius put both his arms around Jayce, gathering him closer so he could place a gentle kiss to the crown of Jayce's head.

He did not need Alexius to say anything. The way Alexius held him and kissed him was all Jayce needed to understand the strength of his feelings.

Jayce closed his eyes and smiled contentedly against his lover's chest.

Chapter
Seventeen

The Knights Tourney arrived on a bright summer's day. The fields outside of town were teeming with people and instead of the droning of dragonflies and birdsong filling the air, it was filled with the sounds of voices and music and announcements being called out from across the three stadiums where each of the three competitions would take place.

Jayce walked alone through the grassy pathways that wound between the tents and stadiums that had been erected all over the place. Around him, bards played their instruments, street performers juggled brightly coloured balls, or acted out comedy routines. Equipment such as swords and even horse panoplies were carried to-and-fro by harried-looking attendants.

Sitting on a rock by one of the stadiums, Jayce spotted an old man with a group of children sitting around him while he told stories of Tourneys from years past.

"The lance bent his helmet nearly clean in half and broke his nose, but that did not stop old Sir Ronauld from getting back up onto his horse."

On his way to the stadium where the duels were soon to take

place, he heard a familiar voice call out his name. "*Jaaayce!*"

He whirled around to see Maple racing towards him. Her red hair was tied into its customary two plaits and she had a flower crown made of daisies sitting slightly askew upon her head. Two girls trailed behind her, also with crowns of daisies in their hair.

"We're going to see if they'll let us pet the horses before the jousting starts," said Maple. "Do you want to come with us?"

"That sounds like fun, but I promised I'd watch Alexius in the duels and it's just about to start."

"My mum said I'm not allowed to watch the duels because they might get stabbed," one of the little girls said miserably.

"Ooh, I want to see that!" said the other.

"I'm sure you could always sneak in and watch it from beneath the stands," Jayce suggested.

"That's a good idea," Maple said. "We'll come watch Alexius stab people after we've petted the horses. Bye Jayce!"

The three girls set off again, racing through the crowd and out of sight. Jayce smiled, thinking it was nice to see Maple spending time with friends that made her happy.

When Jayce finally made it into the second stadium, the seats were almost completely full. He found Iris sitting in one of the front rows.

"You're late," they said, as Jayce took a seat beside them. "You missed Florent in the horse races."

"Sorry," said Jayce, wiping at his brow, which was already beginning to prick with sweat from the glaring sun. "We slept in."

Iris looked at him with narrowed eyes behind their round spectacles. It made Jayce feel as though they could see straight through him and knew of the licentious reasons for why he and Alexius might have gotten out of bed so late on the day of the Tourney.

"How did Florent do in the races?" he asked in an attempt to steer away from the subject.

"He came in second place," Iris said. "I think he was disappointed when he realised you weren't there to see."

There was an odd undercurrent to Iris's tone when they said that last part. Something a bit bitter and . . . sad, maybe?

But Jayce didn't get to linger on it for very long. The duels were about to start.

Eight knights stepped out onto the grounds before the stands to raucous applause and cheer.

All were unfamiliar to Jayce except for two. Alexius was suited up in his rose-gold armour, but instead of a red cape, he wore one that was the colour of gold. Florent wore the same armour of rose-gold as Alexius and the rest of the knights. His cape, however, was of green filigree.

Marie, the daughter of the Grand Duke, stood on the dais swathed in silk awnings and that stood higher than the rest of the stands. She was dressed in an exquisite emerald dress with emerald-coloured ribbons in her pale blonde hair. The dress was just as revealing as the one she had worn the night of the Grand Duke's birthday celebrations.

Oh dear, thought Jayce. *I hope Alexius won't get too distracted.*

Marie started off with welcoming the crowd and introducing herself as the patron for this competition. Next, she began introducing those competing. Sir Pierre of Vonsé. Sir Florent of the Crown City. Sir Fabien of Bassbanier.

And finally, "Sir Alexius of Étoisaint."

The cheers that followed that introduction were perhaps a little more exuberant than the rest, Jayce thought. Iris even whistled.

"Eight knights will fight against one another until eight becomes four and four becomes two and two becomes one. One champion!" said Marie from upon the dais. "During these duels, our knights must fight honourably, and no fatal blow will be struck. The duels will continue until one concedes defeat or falls to their knees. And as is tradition in the duels of the Knights Tourney, our competing brave knights will step forward and make their oaths."

"What are the oaths?" Jayce asked Iris.

"Something the knights swear on as proof they'll perform with honour and chivalry in the Tourney," they explained. "So, if it was me, I might swear on my books. Or Fable."

The first knight stepped forward, Sir Olivier of the newly reclaimed Redvale. He made his oath upon his wife. When he was finished, the next knight took his place and made their oath. Sir Fabien of Bassbanier swore upon Her Majesty, the Queen, for bestowing upon him the honour of knighthood.

When it was Florent's turn to announce his knight's oath, he swore upon his late mother.

Three more knights swore their vows until, finally, it was Alexius's turn. Jayce found himself leaning forward in his seat unconsciously, curious to know what it was Alexius would swear on. His late grandmother or late parents? On his friend Joséphine, the Hero of Solière?

Like the other knights had done, Alexius went to one knee and held the tip of his sheathed sword to the earth, both hands wrapped around the hilt. In a voice that carried clearly throughout the stadium, he said, "I make my solemn oath on the love of Jayce Marken, to uphold the honour of knighthood."

Jayce thought he might have heard a lady's gasp from somewhere behind him and noticed Iris regarding him with more than a little surprise. But he was far too focused on Alexius, who was rising from his kneel, to pay anything else any heed.

Because what else could possibly be more important in that moment than looking at Alexius?

He swore his oath on me. In front of all these people.

Jayce wasn't sure there had ever been a time before now where he wanted so badly to kiss Alexius. If he was in possession of a weaker will, he thought he might have just hurtled over the bannister in front of him and raced across the grounds until he could throw himself into Alexius's arms.

Alexius was the last knight to swear his oath and Jayce was certain he heard a tremor in Marie's voice when she next spoke. "And there you have it. Our brave and honourable knights. Each competing this day for the privilege of being crowned a champion. Now, may the duels begin!"

The first knights to engage in their duel were Florent and Sir Pierre. Soon the stadium was ringing with the sound of sword striking sword and cheers—and even some heckles—from the crowd.

It was a good duel and Jayce realised this was the first time he had ever seen Florent fight. He was a skilled swordsman, not that it came as a surprise. What did surprise Jayce were the similarities between Florent's fighting style and his own. Like Jayce, he moved with quicksilver grace. They both seemed to favour the kind of parries and lunges that were meant to be easy on the wielder, while all the while tiring out the opponent.

Iris seemed to be on the edge of their seat for the whole match. Their fingers curled tightly in their lap. Only when the match was over and Florent was named the victor did Iris seem to unwind. Jayce would even go so far as to say they looked more than a little pleased about Florent's victory.

When it was Alexius's turn to fight against Sir Olivier, it was Jayce who was on edge the whole time. Tensing and wincing whenever it seemed as though Olivier was gaining the upper hand. But in the end, Jayce needn't have worried, for Alexius came out victorious when Sir Olivier admitted defeat.

By the end of the first round, Jayce was itching to pick up a sword of his own—when was the last time he had even held one? He might have to start pestering Alexius for some sparring sessions.

Alexius's next duel was against Florent.

"Well, this should be interesting," said Iris. "Who do you think will win?"

"Do you really need to ask me that?"

"Right. Of course you'll side with the man you're fucking."

"If you want to put it that way, yes," said Jayce.

"Then I suppose I'll put my metaphorical money on Florent," Iris said and hurriedly added, "Just to be fair."

"Of course."

The duel between Florent and Alexius went on for longer than the others had so far. Jayce attributed it to being because both men were quite evenly matched in speed, strength, and overall skill. That, and there seemed to be a hard determination driving both of them. As if losing to the other was the very last thing either of them wanted to do.

Jayce thought he even caught their lips moving during the duel. But it was impossible to tell from this distance what was being said between Alexius and Florent while they exchanged blows.

The duel was finally decided when a misstep, likely from fatigue and culminated with the warmth of the day, caused Florent to stagger and allowed Alexius to use it to his advantage. He rammed his shield into Florent's before the elf had a chance to right his balance and sent him toppling onto his back.

When Alexius held his sword to Florent's neck, Florent dropped his own and said in a loud voice, "I yield."

A pandemonium of cheers erupted in the stands as Alexius was declared the victor of the duels for this year's Tourney.

Alexius extended a hand to help Florent back onto his feet. The two of them clapped each other on the back. A sign of no hard feelings.

"It's a good thing we really weren't betting money then," Iris said over the noise of the crowd. "Or my pockets would be looking a little lighter now."

"Well, if you happened to feel so inclined," said Jayce. "I wouldn't say no."

Iris grumbled a response that was lost to the noise of the crowd.

Later, after he had watched Alexius crowned with the laurels of a Tourney victor and the stadium had emptied out, Iris left to try and find Florent. "Someone has to make sure he isn't going to drown his aching pride in too much beer."

Jayce, meanwhile, had plans to see one person and one

person only.

He found Alexius in one of the tents around the arena. He'd removed the laurel crown from his head and was no longer in armour; he was dressed now in only trousers and a plain, white shirt with the sleeves rolled up to the elbows and the front mostly unlaced and revealing an ample amount of his well-defined chest.

He was sitting on a stool, holding a damp cloth to the back of his neck. When he saw Jayce step in, his expression lit up in a way that made Jayce's chest feel tight.

"Congratulations," he said. "That was quite the performance."

Alexius chuckled. He'd gotten up to meet Jayce in the middle of the tent. "You make it sound like I was out there dancing in front of everyone."

"You as a dancer? Now that would be a sight."

"Excuse you." Alexius sounded mock-affronted. "I would be a remarkable dancer. Audiences would weep at my grace."

Jayce smiled. He felt full to bursting with this happiness welling up inside of him. "I'll believe it when I see it."

Alexius stepped in closer, his head bending slightly over Jayce's, and he lifted one hand to brush his fingertips along Jayce's cheekbone. Jayce had to repress a shiver at the contact.

"'I make my solemn oath on the love of Jayce Marken'?" he said softly, quoting Alexius's oath from earlier.

"You didn't like it?"

"I never said that. I only—Of all the things you could have made your oath on?"

"Because your love means everything to me, Jayce," Alexius said with a heartrending amount of sincerity. "Because there's nothing in this life that I want to honour more than you. Nothing I want to be more worthy of."

Just when Jayce thought that Alexius's words and Alexius himself could not have more of an effect on him, he was proven wrong. He felt struck mute by the sheer inadequacy of anything he could possibly think to say to Alexius in return.

For lack of anything to say, Jayce pushed up instead to meet Alexius's lips with his. Alexius did not hesitate in returning the kiss. One of his arms was already snaking around Jayce's lower back to pull their bodies more closely together.

All Jayce could think about was what exactly had he done to deserve this man? Alexius de Viccarri. Who was good and kind and miraculously in love with Jayce.

When they parted, Jayce stayed close enough that they were still nose to nose. He smirked. "You're very sweaty."

He felt Alexius's warm breath of laughter against his lips. "Yes. Fighting three duels in armour in the hot sun will do that to you."

"You should bathe."

"Maybe you could help me with that?"

Jayce shoved Alexius lightly. "Maybe another time when we're not in a tent that anyone could walk into."

"Right," Alexius said with some disappointment.

"I'm going to see if I can find Iris and Florent. I think the jousting should be about to start soon."

"I'll meet you outside of the stadium?"

Jayce agreed and, with a quick, parting kiss to Alexius's cheek, he left.

As he wound his way past the array of tents—which seemed to have mostly emptied by now—Jayce found his thoughts full of Alexius. Of the feel of his lips and his body against Jayce's. Of the joy he made Jayce feel whenever he was with him.

It was probably for that reason that Jayce never noticed the lone figure approaching him from behind.

The last thing he knew was a blast of pain in the back of his head.

And then nothing.

Chapter
Eighteen

A spiking pain in the back of his skull was the first thing Jayce was aware of as consciousness returned to him. The more awake Jayce became, the more pronounced the pain in his head. He made to lift a hand to touch the spot that was throbbing, only to find that he could not.

His hands were bound.

Awareness flooded back to him in full force.

He was lying on his side on the rough, uneven ground of a forest floor. The sharp points of stones and twigs digging almost painfully into his arm and leg, even through the threads of his clothing. He tried tugging his hands out of the coarse rope that had bound them together behind his back, but it was fruitless. His bindings were too well secured.

"The bitch is finally awake, I see."

Jayce went still.

He knew that gruff voice and that crude nickname all too well.

Peering over his shoulder, Jayce's suspicions were confirmed when he saw none other than Detlas, the huge, former general of the Dark Lord's army, lounging on a moss-covered log behind him.

"Hello Detlas," Jayce said with as much imperiousness as he could muster for someone in his position.

Detlas's mouth curled into a sneer. "Hello Grey."

"I think you'll find that I don't go by that alias anymore."

"I'm sure you don't." Detlas heaved his heavy bulk off the log and took a few, short steps towards Jayce. "If you did, I'm sure the people around here would have finished you off already and I never would have got my chance to make good on that promise I made to you all those months ago. You do remember what one I'm talking about, don't you?"

"I do," said Jayce. "Speaking of our last encounter, how's that wound I gave you?"

The tip of Detlas's boot caught Jayce viciously across the cheekbone. His head snapped to the side and white starbursts popped across his vision as fiery pain exploded beneath his skin.

"Still sore about that, I see," he said, licking at the blood that had trailed down from his split skin to his lips.

Detlas circled around him so he could then place a hefty kick to Jayce's stomach that had him curling in on himself.

The former general reached down and grabbed Jayce by the collar of his tunic. Lifting him somewhat off the ground and bringing their faces close together. Jayce had to force himself not to wince when he got a whiff of Detlas's repugnant breath.

"If I didn't know any better, I never would have guessed that you were Grey," Detlas snarled. "What would the Dark Lord think if he could see you now? His precious protégé playing at being a common peasant."

"It's a good thing I don't really give a damn what he'd think."

Another blow to his face that sent the world spinning before his eyes.

Detlas released his grip on him, and Jayce fell back. The impact was not gentle on his bound hands.

There was a hiss of metal as Detlas pulled a knife from his belt. It was a broad blade with a slightly curved, sharp tip. Designed for piercing and carving through animal hide.

And Jayce couldn't imagine that Detlas was about to pull a deer carcass out of the bush and skin it while he and Jayce exchanged a barbed back and forth.

Detlas touched the tip of the knife to his finger, as if testing its sharpness. "I promised you, the last time we met, that I would make you regret ever betraying us."

The smile he gave Jayce was chilling.

"And I'm about to do just that."

Jayce couldn't be sure about how much time had passed. But by the time Detlas had had enough, Jayce was in possession of an eye that was swelling so rapidly it was growing hard to see out of, the metallic taste of blood in his mouth, and what he was sure was quite a few bruises forming along his body.

And then, of course, there was the knife Detlas had left stuck in his thigh.

It could be worse, he supposed. The knife could have ended up in his heart or his neck.

At some point, throughout the sustained beating, Jayce had somehow ended up propped against the base of a wide oak tree.

Detlas had wandered off a short distance. His broad back turned to Jayce and even with his faculties somewhat clouded by pain, Jayce knew what he had to do. And he had to do it quickly.

Lifting his right leg and leaning his body forward—ignoring the agonised protest that came from his damaged midsection—he took the hilt of the knife between his teeth, and with a swift jerk of his head, pulled it out of his thigh.

The wooden handle helped to muffle any noise of pain that came from him.

Another jerk, and Jayce dropped the knife over his shoulder, catching it awkwardly with his tied hands, blade first. He'd just managed to flip it around so that the point of the edge of the blade was positioned against the rope around his wrists when Detlas finally turned to face him again.

The man's already grubby shirt was now made even filthier with a few blood spatters, creating dark stains on the white fabric.

As Detlas made his way back towards him, Jayce feared that he might notice the knife was missing from the sheath he had made of Jayce's leg.

"So, what exactly do you plan on doing with me?" asked Jayce, in the hope that if he kept Detlas talking, he wouldn't notice much else. "After you're done beating me to a pulp, of course."

"What do you think I'm going to do?" said Detlas. "I'm going to drive my blade straight through you until the dirt runs red with your blood and then dump your traitorous carcass somewhere for the wolves to find."

Jayce tried to keep the movement of his shoulder as minute as possible as he said, "My, my, I had no idea you were capable of such flowery speech, Detlas. And tell me, what do you think killing me is going to accomplish? It's not going to change what's already been done. It won't stop you from being a wanted man in every corner of Solière. And it certainly won't return you to any position of power."

"I'm no fool," Detlas growled. "I understand that killing you won't magically return things to the way they were before you betrayed our master. But I at least want the satisfaction of watching you suffer for your treachery."

"So loyal." Jayce could feel the bonds loosening. Just a little more.

"Unlike you."

"Yes, how terrible of me not to be loyal to the man who stole me from my family, tortured and enslaved me."

"Is that why you betrayed us? Because the Dark Lord took you from a lowly life? How ridiculous. You should have been grateful. He made you into something great. He gave you power."

"Power in exchange for free will?" said Jayce. "I'm not sure even you would be content with being made into a puppet for that, Detlas."

"And what do you know about me?"

"For one thing, you're not particularly observant, are you?"

Before Detlas could respond, Jayce lunged forward, with his hands now free and driving the knife towards Detlas's unprotected chest.

But Detlas was too quick for him. Not being hampered by painful injuries as Jayce was, it was no great feat for Detlas to sidestep Jayce's attack.

Grabbing him by his knife arm, Detlas wrenched the knife out of Jayce's already weakened grip. It fell to the ground and Detlas swung Jayce around before slamming his elbow hard into Jayce's jaw.

The blow knocked Jayce off his feet. He'd barely even hit the ground before Detlas was on top of him, thick hands clamping around his throat.

"Foolish little bitch," Detlas growled as Jayce fought to dislodge the man's choking hold on him. "Did you really think you'd be able to take me out with that pitiful attempt?"

Jayce's vision was beginning to blur. Darkness crept in at the edges.

"Maybe if you still had that power you were so quick to give up, you'd be more of a match for me."

Fuck that, Jayce thought defiantly, as he clawed at some of the leaf litter strewn along the ground. He gathered a bunch of it into his fist and threw it into Detlas's eyes.

The man flinched away. It loosened his hold around Jayce's neck but not all the way, so Jayce brought his knee up harshly between Detlas's legs.

As he thought, it worked like a charm. A pained grunt wrenched itself from Detlas and his hands lifted from Jayce to belatedly defend his abused body part.

Now free, Jayce was able to pull himself from beneath Detlas.

He scrambled for where the knife lay discarded, kicking out when a hand caught him around the ankle, and felt his foot collide with what must have been Detlas's face.

As soon as he picked the knife up in his hands, everything seemed to happen all at once.

When Jayce turned back to face Detlas, lashing out with the blade, he quickly discovered that Detlas was already upon him.

And Jayce's knife had already gone through his neck.

Detlas's eyes went wide, his body frozen. He choked on the blood that poured from his mouth and the wound in the side of his neck. The warmth of it spilled over onto Jayce's hand.

Detlas lifted shaky hands to claw at the one Jayce had around the knife in his neck. Steeling himself, Jayce pulled the knife out of Detlas's neck with a spray of blood, only to then draw it across the man's throat instead.

Jayce saw the life flee rapidly from Detlas's eyes. His heavy frame, now limp, toppled forward and Jayce kicked the body away when it slumped onto him.

Jayce sat there, just staring at the now still body of Detlas and gulping in lungfuls of air for what felt like a long time.

Night was beginning to fall, darkening the world around him and bringing with it a chill in the air. Jayce was injured and in the middle of some forest, how many miles from Étoisaint, he hardly knew. There were no horses in sight, however, so he couldn't imagine they had travelled too far.

He couldn't stay here. The chances that anyone would find him any time soon were slim at best.

Tearing off some of the cloth from Detlas's tunic, Jayce wrapped it tight around the still weeping knife wound. It hadn't been too deep, but nearly the entirety of his left thigh was stained red with his blood, and just looking at it made him feel weak. It was only through sheer force of will that he hauled himself to his feet and began walking—hobbling, more like it—and left Detlas's body behind.

Who's going to be food for the wolves now?

~

It was sometime before Jayce found himself out of the forest and onto a road. By that time, night had taken over the sky completely and the world blurred and swayed dangerously beneath his feet, even when he wasn't walking.

His wounded leg was becoming increasingly difficult to walk on and there was a pain in his ribs that forced his breath out in shallow pants.

Jayce thought he might collapse on the side of the dirt road then and there, but it seemed that good fortune was smiling down on him. No sooner had he stepped out past the tree line, did a horse-drawn cart come trundling by, drawing to a halt in front of him.

A man in a patched brown cloak and a white beard leapt down from the front. "Gods, son," said the man. "What happened to you?"

Jayce did not—could not—reply. He was too busy falling to his knees, as his legs refused to hold him up any longer.

"Hold on." The man was already placing a hand beneath his arms, getting ready to haul him to his feet. "I'll bring you to a physician."

"No," Jayce gasped out. "The . . . de Viccarri estate. Take me there. Do—do you know where it is?"

"The de Viccarri estate? Sure, I know where it is. But you—"

"Please." Jayce had no energy to stifle the pleading in his tone.

The man studied him for just a moment longer before saying, "All right. I'll take you there."

That was the last thing Jayce heard before he blacked out.

He came to once or twice. The sight of the star-speckled sky above greeted him each time, along with a gentle rocking motion and the faint sound of hooves hitting earth. Distantly, he was aware that he must be in the back of the cart.

"Hold on, son," he heard a somewhat familiar voice say to him the second time he woke. "We're almost there."

Jayce passed out.

The third time he regained consciousness, he was aware of multiple voices speaking. One was a woman's and even in his muddled, pain-filled state, he recognised it easily enough. *Estelle.*

Then there came a voice he would know anywhere.

Something shook the cart he was lying on and he soon found himself looking up into a most beloved face.

"Alexius," he said. A wealth of feeling lay behind that one word.

"Jayce." There was emotion in Alexius's voice as he uttered Jayce's name as well.

He felt Alexius take him into his arms and for the fourth time that night, Jayce allowed himself to succumb to oblivion.

Chapter Nineteen

Sunlight was in Jayce's eyes when he awoke.

Or eye.

He quickly discovered that he couldn't quite open his left eye.

His body was stiff and sore, and it did not take long for him to remember why. He also didn't have to think too far back to remember why he was no longer in danger. In the moments before he passed out, he remembered a pair of arms encircling him. Holding him and keeping him safe. The soft bed beneath him now could not compare to how wonderful it felt to be held by Alexius.

He was in his room at the de Viccarri estate. He recognised the abundance of green. Gingerly, Jayce pushed himself into a sitting position, ignoring the way his whole body screeched in protest. He thought he could even feel the rough bite of stitches pulling on his left leg.

Oh, right. I was stabbed there.

The bedroom door opened, and Alexius stepped inside.

He was dressed in plain clothes. His black curls were in a disarray, as if he'd been combing his fingers through them countless times. He looked tired and hollowed out.

That look dissipated once he saw Jayce, awake and sitting up.

"Jayce." The word left him in a breathless rush as he hastened to Jayce's bedside, taking up the chair there that Jayce hadn't noticed before. "Gods, you—Are you all right? How do you feel?"

"I've had better days," said Jayce, reaching to prod at his bottom lip, which he was sure was cut.

"Don't touch it. You'll make it worse." Alexius gently drew Jayce's hand away from his lip and held it on top of the bedsheets between them.

"How are you?" Jayce asked after a pause.

Alexius gave him an incredulous look. "You're asking me how *I* am? I'm not the one who looks as though they've been trampled by a bull!"

That's not too far off from the truth, Jayce almost said, but decided against it. "But you look exhausted. And as if you're about to cry at any moment."

"Because I've been worried about you, you fool! You don't understand how panicked I was when you disappeared like that. And then you just showed up again, all bloody and bruised in the back of some man's cart and when you wouldn't wake up. I—I thought—" Alexius didn't seem capable of continuing. He dropped his head into his free hand and Jayce heard him take in a shuddering breath.

Jayce felt a pang of guilt at having caused Alexius such distress. "I'm here," was all he could think to say, even though it felt woefully insufficient. So he leaned forward, carding his fingers through Alexius's hair until he lifted his head. When he did so, Jayce pressed his lips softly to Alexius's, ignoring the spark of pain from the cut on his lip.

Even when he pulled away, he and Alexius stayed with their heads bent close together, the tips of their noses just barely touching.

Alexius still hadn't let go of his hand.

Finally, Alexius said, "What happened, Jayce?"

So Jayce told him about Detlas, how he managed to snatch Jayce as he was leaving Alexius's tent and brought him out into a forest all to try to get revenge for his betrayal at the Dark Citadel.

"Are you sure he's dead?" Alexius asked him once he was finished speaking.

"Positive."

"Good. I only wish I could have killed him myself."

Jayce thought that the only times he had heard Alexius sound so angry was when they had first met in the Dark Lord's dungeons. And again, during their encounter with the bandits. He'd almost forgotten that Alexius was even capable of feeling such an emotion as anger.

"Are you upset that I didn't give you the chance to be my knight in shining armour?" Jayce teased. "To pull off a daring rescue and sweep me off my feet?"

Alexius let out a weak laugh. "I think you've proven that you hardly need anyone to come to your rescue."

Not true, Jayce thought. *You did rescue me, Alexius. When we first met. And I would not be here without you.*

However, Jayce wasn't sure he was in the mood for voicing such sappy sentiments. Instead, he shuffled over on the bed a bit and patted the space next to him. "I'm not comfortable enough," he said. "Come sit with me."

Alexius looked uncertain. "I'm not sure that's such a good idea. I might accidentally aggravate your injuries."

"I don't care about that."

"But—"

"I'm not made of glass, Alexius. Just—I want you to hold me, all right?"

He didn't mean for the vulnerability to creep into his words, but it seemed to do the trick. Alexius's expression softened, and he rose from his chair to get on the bed beside Jayce. Carefully positioning himself until he was seated comfortably against the headboard with Jayce leaning back against his broad chest. His arms wrapped themselves loosely around Jayce's shoulders.

Contentment settled peacefully over Jayce like a light but warm blanket. Closing his eyes, he turned his head to the side so he could rest it against the crook between Alexius's shoulder and neck, breathing in the scent of him.

He felt Alexius's lips against the crown of his head.

"I love you, Jayce."

"And I love you, Alexius."

~

Recovery was a slow, and frankly annoying, process. None of the wounds Jayce had sustained were incredibly serious. Even the knife wound in his leg had been clean and, apart from a scar, would heal with no permanent damage. But he was still confined to his bed much of the time for the next few days and forced to rely on the help of Alexius and the house staff. He could not even make it to the bathroom without someone to lean against.

Of course, this meant Jayce was not able to work at *Tails and Tomes* for a while, and it wasn't long before he found himself missing the cosy store and the smell of old books and booklice repellent. Iris did come to visit him a few times, even bringing Fable along with them. The cat stayed curled up in Jayce's lap the whole time.

"She's been missing you," Iris told him.

Iris and Fable weren't Jayce's only visitors. Florent also stopped by and with a new poetry book that he offered to spend the day reading to Jayce. Jayce accepted the offer, if only to see Alexius's face take on a somewhat strained quality.

Maple and her mothers also came to visit him, bearing delicious baked goods and a **Feel Better Soon** note from Maple.

And throughout it all, Alexius was never far from his side. He'd even gone as far as to take leave from work so he could remain with Jayce, fetch him water when he needed, change the bandaging around his leg, even helping him to bathe.

One night, the two of them soaked together in the bath, with Jayce leaning back against Alexius, while he rubbed a bar of soap up and down Jayce's arm with soothing, attentive motions.

"Perhaps you should hang up your sword and armour," said Jayce, watching Alexius work the soap in between his fingers. "Become a nurse instead."

"I'm sure nurses don't take care of their patients in such an *intimate* way as this." Alexius trailed the soap slowly down Jayce's bare torso.

Jayce bit at the inside of his cheek. "Hm. I suppose I would get rather jealous if you were bathing anyone else like this."

Alexius laughed softly and pressed his face into the back of Jayce's wet hair. "This special treatment is for you only."

Jayce closed his eyes and smiled. "Lucky me."

Chapter
Twenty

"Stop biting your nails."

"I'm not."

"Yes, you are, Jayce. I can clearly see you biting them."

"Hmph."

"Don't get in a bad mood with me." Even with the admonishment, there was laughter in Alexius's voice. And fondness. Always fondness when he spoke to Jayce. "You were the one who just got caught in a lie."

Jayce shot him a withering glare from the opposite seat of the carriage. "Shut up."

"Scary," Alexius said with a dimpled grin. Then, more seriously, "There's no need to be nervous, you know?"

"Easy for you to say," said Jayce, turning to watch the sprawling green countryside roll by outside the carriage window.

He felt Alexius lean across to take one of his hands in his own. Jayce drew his gaze away from the window to look at Alexius, who was looking at him in turn with such a loving expression that Jayce felt disarmed by it.

"I'm telling you; you have nothing to worry about. She's going to be so happy to see you."

Hesitantly, Jayce said, "How can you be so sure?"

"Because I have a good feeling about it."

Jayce scoffed.

"*And,*" Alexius added, "Because I know you. Because you're impossible not to love."

"You are . . . embarrassingly sappy," said Jayce.

Alexius flashed him that bright smile of his that could rival the sun. "Unrepentantly."

It wasn't long before the carriage came to a halt and Guillaume signalled that they had arrived.

Stepping out, Jayce saw that they had stopped out the front of a small cottage with a red roof, surrounded by an apple orchard. Simple and picturesque. It was lovely and inviting, yet Jayce felt a lump in his throat just looking at it.

"Are you ready?" Alexius asked, sidling up beside him.

No, Jayce wanted to say. But he thought it would sound ridiculous. He had been Grey for almost as long as he could remember. The second most feared man in all of Solière. He had fought against armies and slain a drake as tall as a mountain. This should not be something that instilled fear in him. And yet . . .

"I'm not the boy she would remember, if she even remembers me at all," he said. "I've done terrible things. I'm . . . ."

"None of that matters right now," Alexius said softly. "There will be time to talk and make her understand later. But first, you need to walk up to that house and knock on the door." He slipped his hand into Jayce's, giving it a reassuring squeeze.

Jayce squeezed back, infinitely grateful to have Alexius by his side.

Hand in hand, he and Alexius walked up the dirt track towards the cottage. All too soon, they were standing in front of the door, painted a green that was cracked and peeling in places.

Jayce raised a closed fist, hesitated, mustered his resolve, and finally knocked.

It took a couple of moments before there was the sound of

approaching footsteps on the other side and the door opened to reveal a tall, drakekin with dull blue scales. He was leaning heavily on a wooden cane.

He looked mildly surprised to see Jayce and Alexius standing before him, before offering a polite smile. "Hello. Can I help you?"

"Yes," said Jayce. "Could you please tell me where I can find—"

There was a booming bark from behind them, and Jayce looked around in time to be bowled over by a brown bear of a dog. Thankfully, Alexius had moved to catch him from being completely knocked to the ground.

"Fang, no," the drakekin said in despair. "I'm so sorry. He's not usually like this."

Jayce pulled away enough from having his face slobbered all over so he could look the dog in the face. It had droopy yellow eyes and a droopy muzzle with a great pink tongue lolling out. It almost looked like it was smiling. The last time he had seen this dog, it had been a much smaller pup.

"Fang," Jayce said, and smiled. "I know you."

The dog let out a whining sound and continued licking Jayce's face and trying to climb on top of him.

"Mathéo, Fang just came racing up to the house all of a sudden. What's—"

A woman had stepped out from behind one of the rows of apple trees. She was short and plump, carrying a wicker basket filled with apples. He imagined her skin might have been fair once, before long days working in the sun had darkened it to a light brown. Her long hair was tied into a knot at the back of her head. Although threaded with grey, it was the same blue-black as Jayce's and her eyes were the same aqua blue.

"Yara, dear?" the drakekin sounded concerned. "What is it?"

His mother had gone stone-still the moment she laid eyes on him.

Pushing Fang back, Jayce pulled himself to his feet, with some help from Alexius.

She looked at him as if he were some sort of apparition. Like she could not believe what was right in front of her, but so desperately wanted to. "Is it . . . is it really you?" Her voice was trembling. Tears were already preparing to spill.

Jayce felt like a deer caught by the hounds. His head was a jumble of panicked thoughts. What was he supposed to say? What was he supposed to do?

Only when he felt a gentle pressure at his back—Alexius's hand—urging him forward was he able to find his voice.

"Mother . . . I'm home."

The dam collapsed. A wordless cry escaped his mother's lips and the basket of apples fell to the ground as she rushed forward until Jayce was in her arms.

Tears fell, and not just on his mother's part. He could feel them running down his own cheeks without his consent.

"My boy," his mother kept chanting between sobs, stroking the back of his head. "My boy. I finally have my boy back."

The rest of the day was spent in joyful reunion. Jayce's mother seemed adamant not to let him out of her sight for a single moment, as if he would disappear into the air like a cloud of smoke the moment she did.

He was introduced to Mathéo, his mother's husband of five years. His stepfather, who—oddly enough—seemed almost as euphoric as his mother to have Jayce returned to them, despite never having met each other before.

Jayce, in turn, introduced them to Alexius, and he might as well have been announcing their impending marriage with the amount of fuss that was made.

There were still many things that went unsaid that day. Things that he wished to speak about with his mother alone, first. And Jayce would do that tomorrow. For now, he would simply enjoy this.

Later that night, he and Alexius found themselves laying on the couch together, his mother and Mathéo having long since gone to bed. Fang was curled up on the rug beside the couch, snoring. The dog had been just as reluctant to part from Jayce's side.

He could feel a draft blowing in from the window across the living room, but with Alexius's arms wrapped around him and his head resting against Alexius's chest, Jayce could not bring himself to care.

He knew Alexius wasn't asleep, which was why he said, "I want to join the Mercenaries Guild."

Alexius went still. "What?"

"I want to join the Mercenaries Guild," he repeated simply.

"I know what you said, I just—" Alexius shifted, propping himself up on his elbows, so he could look down at Jayce. "What brought this on?"

Jayce sat up as well. "I've been thinking about it for a while now. Before the Tourney, I saw someone post a recruitment notice in town. I spoke with her, and she told me about the guild's new mission to provide aid to those who need it. And I thought—well, it sounds perfect for me."

"So, you've already decided? But . . . what about the bookshop?"

"I . . . I am fond of the shop and I'm grateful to Iris for giving me employment, but I want more from life than stacking shelves and sitting behind a counter," Jayce explained. "I want to do more to make amends for all the things I have done."

"None of that was your fault, Jayce," said Alexius. "The Dark Lord was controlling you."

"I know, I know that, but—could you please understand that even with the collar around my neck, it still doesn't absolve me of my guilt? Because it was still by my hand that people died. Lost their loved ones and had their homes taken from them. If you were in my place, would you not still feel some sense of responsibility?"

There was a furrow between Alexius's brows. "Of course I would," he admitted almost reluctantly. "But that means you won't be staying in Étoisaint anymore . . . I won't get to see you."

He looked so much like a sad puppy that Jayce couldn't keep the smile off his face. Nor could he keep himself from swooping forward to press a delighted kiss to Alexius's lips.

"You'll still get to see me," he said, keeping the distance between himself and Alexius small. "It's not as if I'll be gone forever."

"But I really love having you close to me all the time."

Jayce chuckled. "Ah, now you're sounding more like a spoiled child of wealth."

Alexius made a mock noise of outrage and wrapped his arms around Jayce. They were both laughing now as Jayce fell back onto the couch with Alexius on top of him, planting kisses all over his face and neck.

When Alexius pulled back to look at him, there was a sombre look in his dark eyes. One hand cradled Jayce's face.

"Just . . . Promise me you'll always come back to me safe and whole."

Jayce knew there was no way to keep such a promise, not in the line of work he was seeking. It was inevitable that he would take on dangerous jobs that would lead to injuries. Alexius must have known that, too. He wasn't naïve.

Still, he found himself reaching up to run his fingers along the strong line of Alexius's jaw, already growing rough with stubble. "I promise."

They shared a smile, and then they shared a kiss.

The future was full of uncertainties. It was exciting and intimidating all at the same time. But no matter what the future brought, Jayce vowed to himself that he would do everything in his power to hold on to this. Onto this bright and wondrous thing in his life that made him ache and burn and, most importantly, made him *happy*. Happier than he ever thought he could possibly be.

So long as Alexius wanted him by his side, Jayce would always come back to him.

.

Acknowledgements

Once upon a time, I said I could never write a low-stakes book. That I love high-stakes stories too much. But look at me now.

As always, my profoundest thanks to the beta-readers who helped shape this book into what it is today. To the friends and fellow indie authors who encouraged and advised me as I looked to try new things on this publishing journey. To Jan and Beau for creating the most perfect book cover I could ever have hoped for, for this little book of mine. And of course, to all the readers who have supported *Of Knights and Books and Falling In Love.* Whether that be by purchasing a copy or simply sharing a post about it online. The support of readers is an incredibly powerful thing to us authors, and I cannot even begin to express my gratitude to those of you have offered it to any one of my books.

About the author

Rita A. Rubin is an Australian born author who currently resides in Melbourne and is living her best introvert life. When not writing, Rita can be found with her nose in a book, or PS4 console in her hands or making up ballads to sing to her dog and cat.

Follow Rita on Twitter @ritacoolbeans and Instagram @ritarubin9.

www.ingramcontent.com/pod-product-compliance
Lightning Source LLC
Chambersburg PA
CBHW020008140726
47904CB00018B/2123